D0374451

ANNIE MOORE

FIRST IN LINE FOR AMERICA

First published in 1999 by
Marino Books
an imprint of Mercier Press
16 Hume Street Dublin 2
Tel (01) 661 5299; Fax (01) 661 8583
Trade enquiries to CMD Distribution
55A Spruce Avenue Stillorgan Industrial
Park Blackrock County Dublin

© Eithne Loughrey 1999

ISBN 1 85635 245 5

10 9 8 7 6 5 4 3 2 1

A CIP record for this title is available
from the British Library

This book is sold subject to the
condition that it shall not, by way of
trade or otherwise, be lent, resold,
hired out or otherwise circulated
without the publisher's prior consent
in any form of binding or cover other
than that in which it is published and
without a similar condition including
this condition being imposed on the
subsequent purchaser.

No part of this publication may be
reproduced or transmitted in any
form or by any means, electronic or
mechanical, including photocopying,
recording or any information or
retrieval system, without the prior
permission of the publisher in writing.

Cover design by
Penhouse Design Group
Printed in Ireland by ColourBooks
Baldoyle Industrial Estate, Dublin 13

ANNIE MOORE

FIRST IN LINE FOR AMERICA

EITHNE LOUGHREY

MERCIER PRESS

ACKNOWLEDGEMENTS

Thanks are due to the following for their help while researching and writing this book: Cobh Heritage Centre who kindly sent me all the information about Annie Moore that they had on their files; Jeff Dosik, librarian at the Statue of Liberty-Ellis Island Museum, who supplied me with information from the American side; the National Library of Ireland, who dug up newspapers and official documents relating to the period; the Maritime Museum in Dun Laoghaire, who helped inform me about trans-atlantic vessels of the time; the Tenement Museum in New York's Lower East Side, where I learned a lot about how Annie might have lived in nearby Monroe Street; those friends who kindly 'surfed the Net' to find useful information for me about the period; my publisher Jo O'Donoghue and my editor Rachel Sirr of Marino Books for their help and enthusiasm; and finally, to my husband John, who encouraged me every step of the way.

For my daughter Dara, one of the many who followed in Annie's footsteps and is now living happily in Arizona

CONTENTS

INTRODUCTION

This is the story of Annie Moore – a young Cork girl who emigrated to the United States from Queenstown (now Cobh) in December 1891 with her two younger brothers to join their parents, who had sailed three years earlier.

Anyone who has visited the excellent Heritage Centre in Cobh, County Cork, which houses the permanent 'Queenstown Story' exhibition, will have seen Jeanne Rynhart's life-size sculpture of Annie Moore and her brothers outside the entrance. A similar sculpture by this artist has been erected in the Ellis Island Museum in New York.

Why is Annie Moore commemorated in this way?

Annie Moore arrived in America on 1 January 1892 – the very day of her fifteenth birthday – after a ten-day voyage across the Atlantic. But the reason she stands out from the millions of other immigrants who sailed into New York Harbour is that she was the first immigrant of any nationality to set foot on American soil at the new Immigrant Landing Station on Ellis Island, which was officially opened on the day of her arrival. To celebrate the occasion she was presented with a $10 gold piece by welcoming dignitaries, a fact which was reported in the

New York newspapers of the day as well as in the *Cork Examiner*. Annie Moore was truly 'first in line for America' at Ellis Island. Some twelve million immigrants, of which 580,000 were Irish, were to pass through this immigration station in the subsequent six decades.

With such an auspicious start in the New World, Annie Moore is symbolic of a new wave of immigrants. She made her voyage some forty years after the Famine and although she was poor she wasn't destitute. She travelled in a modern steamship in relative comfort, even as a steerage passenger – a far cry from the plight of those who sailed in the famine ships.

After being united with their parents, the Moore children went off to their new home at 32 Monroe Street, in the Lower East Side of New York City. Further information about the family is somewhat sketchy. The names of Ellen King, Mike Tierney and John and Mary Ryan were all listed as fellow-passengers on the ship's manifest for the S.S. *Nevada* on that voyage, and I have taken the liberty of casting all of them as characters in my story. This book is largely a work of fiction and, as such, a personal interpretation of how Annie and her brothers might have lived in turn-of-the-century New York.

The unveiling of the Annie Moore sculpture in Cobh, County Cork by former President Mary Robinson in February 1993 coincided with the opening of the Cobh Heritage Centre. Indeed the sculpture, created by well-known Irish sculptor Jeanne Rynhart, won the ICI Commemorative Sculpture Award. The idea of commemorating Annie Moore, however, was first conceived by the Irish American Cultural Institute in New York. With official endorsements from the U.S. and Irish governments, a similar sculpture by the same artist was erected on Ellis Island to coincide with the Centennial and Rededication of Ellis Island in 1992. This sculpture was also unveiled by Mary Robinson. These parallel projects are seen as a fitting tribute to the millions of immigrants who followed in Annie's footsteps.

1

NEW HORIZONS

Annie thought she'd be trampled to death in the crush as the passengers surged up the narrow gangplank and scrambled to find space on deck. Holding fast to her small trunk with one hand, she kept a grip on Philip with the other. Ahead she could see Anthony's red head bobbing up and down as, laden with baggage and rolled-up bedding, he pushed his way to the rail on the leeward side of the tender to catch a last glimpse of their aunt and uncle.

'Over here, Annie, I've found a place,' he called.

With one heave, Annie and Philip broke free from the body of the crowd and joined their brother. The noise was overwhelming. The roar of the engines and the mournful hooting of the horn drowned out even the screaming gulls. Pandemonium reigned on board the tender just as it had on the quayside earlier. Porters pushed and swore as they carted enormous boxes of provisions on board. Steerage passengers were shoved aside as the few first-class passengers were escorted on board for the short trip out to the steamer, which was lying at anchor at the mouth of Queenstown harbour.

'All aboard, all aboard,' yelled the steward through a loud hailer.

A wave of panic swept over Annie as her eyes scanned the figures on the quayside. The wan faces all looked the same in the morning light. The train remained there right beside the quay, its tall, narrow funnel still gently belching smoke, although all passengers from Cork had long since disembarked. She could see the horses and carts, having dispatched their cargo, leaving the dockside and trundling up the narrow road towards the town. Tears blinded her. Shivering, she pulled her two young brothers closer, her tears falling on Anthony's tight red curls. The boys clung to her gratefully, silenced for once.

Suddenly there was a mighty clang as the gangplank was pulled up and the rails secured; then they were pulling away from the quay wall. All eyes on board looked their last on the waving hands and stricken faces of the loved ones left behind.

To those departing on board that tender, Queenstown had never looked more splendid than it did on that cold December morning. Lit by the pale winter sun, the imposing new cathedral seemed to give the passengers a parting blessing from the hill. The houses, rising in exuberant terraces from sea level, seemed to look beyond them out to sea, as if they had already let them go. Wisps of smoke rising from the chimneys merged with the long trail of black smoke left by the tender as it moved out beyond Spike Island.

The faces gradually became distant specks, and the passengers fell silent, cowed by the looming shape ahead.

The Guion Royal and United States mail steamer, the SS *Nevada*, lay at the entrance to the harbour waiting to take them on board. Far above them the letters SS *Nevada* stood out boldly from a blinding white background.

Looking up, Annie thought the steamer the most heart-stopping sight she'd ever seen. Suddenly her spirits lifted. 'Look boys,' she cried, turning them around to face it, 'isn't that a grand ship that's taking us to America?'

Charlie and Norah Twomey waved till they could no longer distinguish the forlorn little group waving from the tender as it drew away from them and moved out into the harbour. Charlie, his arm protectively around his wife's shoulders, drew her away from the quay and guided her towards the entrance to the railway station. 'Annie will look after the boys, Norah, don't you fret,' he soothed.

Norah struggled to hold back the tears. 'She will. I know they'll be all right. It's just ... they looked so lonely Charlie. It's such a long way. Besides, I'm sorry to be letting them go, I'd got so fond of them all.' At this she broke down and cried openly, overcome with loneliness already for the children who had been like her own for the past three years.

'I know that, dearest, but it's best for children to be with their own parents, and now that Annie is getting so grown-up and all, 'tis more fitting that Matt and Mary tend to her.'

Norah smiled a little at that. Annie had indeed become a handful in the last year. Just turning fifteen, she was tall for her age and strikingly pretty, with thick auburn hair almost reaching her waist. Wide hazel eyes looked out of a strong face with high cheekbones and a rosy complexion. She had already been marked out as the 'prettiest girl in Shandon', and her outgoing personality and sense of humour meant that she was also one of the liveliest. Besides, she had a saucy way with her and it wasn't a minute too soon for her to be under the firm guiding eye of her own parents, Norah thought.

Annie and her two young brothers had lived with their aunt Norah and uncle Charlie in Chapel Street in Shandon since their parents and older brother Tom had left for America to earn their fortune nearly three years before. They were to stay in Shandon until such time as their parents had made a home for them in New York. Annie had thought her heart would break when her parents had departed Queenstown. She was afraid she would never set eyes on them again. Letters had been frequent enough, however, to reassure her that they were managing quite well and living in what was called the Lower East Side of New York City, and while they had not exactly made their fortune, they had, through determination and sheer hard work, already improved their circumstances.

'I miss you all,' wrote her mother, Mary Moore. 'It will be grand when you come out here to join us. Be patient and Father will book your passage as soon as he can.'

From Mother's letters Annie had gleaned enough about life in New York for it to sound exciting, even frightening. Mary told of the huge crowds of people everywhere – many of them speaking strange languages – the trains that ran high above street level, all filled to overflowing with people coming and going from factories and offices, and the long lines of carriages and horse cars on the city streets.

She described too the splendour of the buildings and the fine parks, the long elegant tree-lined avenues where the gentry lived, and the stylish shops, which were on a scale that she had never seen in her life. Mother explained that these 'department stores' stocked everything a body could need but only the gentry could afford to buy there. Fashionable ladies would arrive at Macy's – a bit like Cash's only a million times bigger – and leave their private carriages waiting while they spent hours getting fitted out for 'the season'. 'They must have dresses for every occasion,' Mother told them, 'ball dresses, walking dresses, travelling dresses, evening robes and even dresses for the garden.'

For all the splendour of life in America as described in Mother's letters, Annie sensed that her parents were experiencing a different kind of existence in this city so far across the ocean. She guessed that a very real home-sickness lay beneath the enthusiastic accounts of the doings of the rich and famous and that the reality of her parents' lives was far from glamorous. Father had found a job in a shirt factory and Mother, after initially working as a domestic help for a wealthy old lady who had since died, had recently got work taking in sewing at which she toiled day and night. Tom, Annie's older brother, worked as a 'bell hop' in a big hotel – that meant a junior porter, according to Uncle Charlie – and hoped to be promoted to porter after a couple of years. Indeed, reading between the lines Annie reached the conclusion that all her parents did was work.

Nonetheless, the letters imparted a sense of excitement and adventure that made Uncle Charlie and Auntie Norah envious and made the children look forward to their future in the New World. Norah and Charlie Twomey were a relatively young couple, not long married. As yet they had no family of their own and so were only too happy to take Annie and her brothers under their wing until it was time for them to join their parents. Norah was proud of her niece's good looks and bright personality and treated her like a younger sister. Anthony and Philip were a lively pair and greatly enjoyed by their Uncle Charlie, who brought them road bowling on Sunday mornings, or down to see the foreign ships anchored along the quays, and even bathing in Crosshaven in summer.

Of late, Annie had really been blossoming. She had a fine singing voice and had recently been taking piano lessons with Miss Dwyer, who said she showed unusual promise. She spent a lot of her spare time in the home of her friend Julia Donohue, who lived nearby and, like Annie, attended the local convent school. Julia came from a large family and Mrs Donohue always made Annie feel like a part of it, not like a visitor the way you felt in most people's homes.

Life was full and Annie was happy. So it came as something of a shock when a letter from her father to Aunt Norah arrived in November, announcing that passage had been booked for Annie and the boys on the SS *Nevada*, scheduled to leave Queenstown on 21 December and arrive in New York on New Year's Day 1892 – Annie's fifteenth birthday! Three tickets were enclosed, leaving no doubt about the reality of this unexpected news.

The boys were enthralled. Aged eleven and seven, they could only see this development as a marvellous adventure, something to really look forward to. Meanwhile, they got on with life as usual. Annie was thrilled and a little frightened by turns. On the one hand, she longed to be reunited with her parents and her older brother. On the other, she didn't want to be torn from the comfort and enjoyment of her present life and catapulted into the unknown. Her head was full of questions. What kind of life would she have in America? Would her parents have changed much?

Annie spent the remaining weeks dreading the upheaval. She'd miss Christmas with her aunt and uncle and the party at Donohue's on St Stephen's Day. What kind of Christmas would it be on board a big ship out on the ocean with lots of people she didn't even know? Dark doubts assailed her when she was alone in bed at night, although outwardly she showed only enthusiasm as she helped Norah to prepare their belongings. After all, Father and Mother were longing to see their children again. Father even mentioned in the letter that they hoped very much that the children would arrive on the very day of Annie's fifteenth birthday so they could all have an even bigger celebration.

Annie's misgivings had to be put aside during her final days at home in any case, as they hastened to get everything ready. Goodbyes had to be said and presents purchased for her parents and for Tom. Mother had requested little things which just couldn't be found in New York for all its grand shops! Could Auntie Norah please send some Keating's cough lozenges for Tom who suffered from a bad chest and some Albion milk and sulphur soap for herself, and oh, how they longed for drisheen from the English Market off the Grand Parade or some butter from the much-missed Butter Market in Shandon, but they knew such things could never survive the journey across the Atlantic.

Despite Annie's apparent enthusiasm, Norah could see that her young niece had mixed feelings and tried to reassure her. 'You'll love it there, Annie. It's the land of plenty. You'll get on and make just as many friends as you have here. And you can write and tell us all about it. Maybe we'll go there some day too.'

'Oh, might you, Auntie?' cried Annie, her eyes widening with delight. 'That would be marvellous.'

That prospect helped to distract her for a while. Auntie Norah had made her think that perhaps the world wasn't as big as she had been imagining, Maybe, after all, it would be a great life. If they could only all stay together, surely no misfortune could befall them.

2

FINDING THEIR SEA LEGS

By the time Annie climbed into her bunk on board the steamer that first night, her mind was awash with impressions of a day different to any she'd experienced before. Feelings of loneliness and apprehension had almost immediately been swept aside by the events of the day. It hadn't even been possible to get out to the decks until the vessel was well under way, and the last Annie saw of her native land was the lighthouse at Mizen Head. Life on board ship, she and her brothers were soon to discover, was as busy as a fair day in Macroom.

Getting on board the steamer from the tender was made easier for Annie and her brothers by a pleasant-looking young man who appeared at her elbow as they drew level with the massive vessel and effortlessly lifted her trunk and placed it on his shoulders. Then he tucked her rolled-up bedding under his other arm and smiled at her. 'You look after them,' he gestured towards the boys. He appeared to have almost no luggage himself, and as they waited to go on board he explained that he had emigrated to the United States some years previously and had only returned briefly to Ireland for his brother's ordination. 'My name is Mike Tierney,' he told her. 'I work in New York City – I'm a tailor.'

Annie looked at him with a mixture of curiosity and admiration. He seemed so sure of himself. 'We're going out there to be with our parents,' she explained shyly, adding, 'We haven't seen them for a few years.'

Then the crowd began to surge forwards and further conversation was impossible. As soon as they were on board, Mike Tierney deposited her luggage at her feet.

'I'm in the men's quarters. I probably won't see you on board at all. So I wish you good luck.' He smiled and was gone as quickly as he had appeared at her side only a short while earlier.

'Let me see your passage tickets, Miss.' A burly young steward stopped Annie and the boys. All passengers were being directed to their accommodation by watchmen placed on each deck. Although the numbers of their berths were clearly marked on their passage tickets, Annie was repeatedly questioned about the boys, especially Anthony. What age were they? Where were their parents? Was she sure her brothers shouldn't be berthing in the men's section? It was only later in the voyage that she learned how strict the authorities were about segregating men from women on board. Even boys of just twelve years of age had to be separated from their womenfolk unless they were placed in family accommodation with their parents.

Having finally persuaded the authorities that Anthony was only eleven, Annie and the boys were directed to their quarters. Down and down they went, descending steep, dark staircases, hauling their heavy baggage with them. Having trudged for what seemed like miles through a labryinth of passageways, the little group eventually reached a large open area, aft of the lower deck, with the women's sleeping quarters at one side and the married couples' accommodation at the other side of the deck. They were directed to a large dormitory which they would share with twenty women of different ages and half a dozen or so other children. Most had boarded the ship at Liverpool and were already well settled in.

Annie was relieved to find herself allotted bunks beside a friendly young woman from Waterford whom she'd already noticed on board the tender. Ellen King, she would find out, was headed for Nebraska, where she was to join her two older sisters and their families. Ellen had been touched by the sight of the brave little trio at Queenstown and now she hastened to their assistance. 'Here, let me help you. Perhaps the boys could take the two top bunks,' she said, while helping to relieve Annie of the baggage.

'Thank you ever so much,' replied Annie, breathless from juggling everything. She wasn't in the least dismayed by the rows of bunk beds. She'd heard worse about travelling steerage in the old days. Uncle Charlie had often regaled them with stories of the dreadful conditions experienced by emigrants who'd gone out to America in the sailing ships directly after the Famine. His mother had family who'd made the trip in 1849 in a sailing ship and barely lived to tell the tale. The overcrowded conditions, the lack of proper sanitary facilities, the smell of sickness and unwashed bodies and clothing, along with the constant roll of the ship for weeks on end, had ensured a nighmarish voyage. No wonder they never came back to Ireland, Annie often thought.

But nowadays of course they had the steamships, the greatest invention in the world, Uncle Charlie called them, and regardless of the direction of the wind, they would steam across to America at a cracking pace – unlike the three or four weeks it used to take in the sailing ships. All going well, Annie and the boys would arrive in the United States of America in ten days' time – New Year's Day. What a birthday that would be!

Before they even had time to unpack their bedding rolls and lay them on their bunks, a stout, bustling woman bore down upon them and whisked them away for a medical examination by the ship's Sanitary Officer. A kindly man of fifty-odd years, he asked them all about their life in Cork and their family in America as he peered into their ears and mouths and listened to their chests with a stethoscope. 'Sound as a bell,' he remarked after he'd examined each one of them. 'You'll have no problems when you get to Ellis Island.'

As they were returning to their quarters, they heard the melancholy sound of the ship's horn announcing departure and became aware of the vibrations of the engines as the SS *Nevada*, like a stately iceberg, glided slowly and majestically towards the open seas.

By the time they'd made up their beds, with the help of Ellen and an older, motherly woman, it was time to unpack the tin mugs and plates that every passenger was instructed to bring on board and follow the others to the dining hall.

Tables stretched down the centre of the room as far as the eye could see. They all had raised wooden edges which Annie soon discovered were to prevent food being thrown to the floor when the ship was on the high seas. Big red-faced men in white aprons and tall white hats stood over steaming cauldrons ladling out food. After queuing patiently with the other passengers, Annie and the boys were finally given mugfuls of hot beef soup and plenty of bread and butter and hastened to join Ellen at table. They found her sitting with a fresh-faced young couple who had also joined the ship at Queenstown. John and Mary Ryan from Skibbereen turned out to be heading for Minnesota, where John's brother had already found work on the railways. John told them that he hoped to get work there too, and soon they were all exchanging life histories and chatting like old friends.

So it was a merry and excited little group that tucked into their first meal aboard the SS *Nevada* as she headed out into the Atlantic on that sunny winter day in 1891. As the low, purplish, winter-clad hills of West Cork slipped away from them, so too did all the apprehension and anxiety of the past few days. The prospect of the voyage ahead settled easily on them, and the novelty of their surroundings distracted them from the momentous step they were taking into the unknown.

Written on board the SS *Nevada*, Christmas Eve 1891

Dear Uncle Charlie and Auntie Norah

I hope you are well and aren't too lonely without us. I thought it best to write to you now and tell you what kind of life it is out on the ocean and also so I won't forget to tell you all about it before I get to New York and begin my new life.

Me and the boys were sad saying goodbye but we forgot about it when we arrived out at the ship. What a surprise. I never saw such a big ship – it stretched up into the sky above us. I wish you could see inside; it is like a big town where people live on long narrow streets and where everyone eats together at long, long tables with pillars here and there like in the Opera House. Only we haven't eaten very much in the last few days because we have been so seasick .

It was terrible hearing everyone moaning and the children crying. I wanted to die. There have been terrible storms, the waves are frightening and rock the boat from side to side. Sometimes we thought we would be thrown out of bed.

But everything is getting better since we awoke this morning and Anthony has already gone up on deck with Mr Ryan, a very nice man from Skib. He and his wife Mary are going out to join his brother and he hopes to get a job on the railways.

Ellie King, who is twenty-one and comes from County Waterford, is going out to her sisters in

Nebraska. She sleeps in the bunk beside us and is very kind to us.

I met a really helpful man from Tipperary on the tender on the way out. He's a tailor and works in New York but came home for his brother's ordination. He's called Mike Tierney and he helped us carry our baggage on board but we won't see him again because he's in the men's quarters at the other end of the ship.

I can't believe that tomorrow is Christmas Day. It's surely the strangest Christmas any of us ever had. I'm thinking of you roasting the goose and of all the excitement at Donohue's but we're not really lonely as everything here is so different. We heard that there will be a Christmas party tomorrow night and we're looking forward to it.

Christmas Night at Eleven O'Clock

This is the longest letter I've ever written but I have so much to tell you about our new life out on the waves of this great Atlantic Ocean. It was such good luck that those waves were not quite as high as usual today and that we all feel much better, and as Mr Ryan says – we've got our sea legs. The boys are fit as fiddles now and played 'buckets' on deck with Mr Ryan and some of the other men yesterday. After tea Ellie helped me put up my hair and arranged it very prettily with a velvet ribbon and I helped her sew some ribbon around the hem of her dress. She says I look nearly as grown up as her with my hair up.

She says that in America, the ladies wear combs in their hair with real jewels in them and put their hair up in a style called a 'pompadour'. It must be really fine. I will learn to do it too and have my picture taken especially to send to you so you can see your fine American niece.

We awoke at six o'clock this morning and you never heard such a rustling as the boys opened their presents. I had to keep mine till last as I tried to shush them. But nobody scolded them because it was Christmas. What excitement when Philip saw the box of conjurer's tricks. He's been playing with them all day and tells us he will make a fortune in America.

Nor do I have to tell you how much Anthony likes the ship model set, all the more so now that he's travelling on one just like the one on the cover of the box. The boxes of dates and sweets looked so good we wanted to open them right away but decided to wait and share them out later on.

I love my warm muff and it will come in very useful here when we take a walk on deck because even when the sun shines, it's so very cold. The red velvet sash is perfectly fine with my blue dress. But the best of all was the book of Irish songs. Thank you, thank you from us all.

It was a great day and the refectory was decorated gaily with coloured paper lanterns and holly and ivy. We all walked on deck in the morning and for the first time I saw how they play buckets. What fun it is. I intend wasting no time but will get Mr Ryan to teach me. The boys play it quite well already.

There was ham for dinner which was good but we all thought about the goose and how Uncle Charlie would be carving it. We would have died for a slice of it. There was even a piece of Christmas pudding for everyone so we have no reason to complain but tonight I think of you all and miss you so much and I hope you are thinking of us.

After dinner we all tried to have a rest before the party but try as I would, my eyes would not stay shut. Well it was the greatest fun of all with singing and dancing.

Mr Ryan played the harmonica and another man from Limerick had an accordion and we danced and sang and played charades. How I wished for Donohues' piano so I could have played a few tunes. They have one upstairs in the first-class saloon but we are not allowed go up there. But we could hear the music and guess the gentry are having fun too, although not, I'm sure, as much as us.

Ellie and I sang 'Oft in the Stilly Night' and everybody joined in and then cheered afterwards. It was like the parish concert. It was a good Christmas night after all. I'm in bed now but not sleepy yet. I have so much to think about: the voyage and the ship and all the passengers and why they are all going to America; about the same stars twinkling down on all of us – out here on the ocean, in Cork and in America. I try to imagine what New York will be like and how different it will be from Cork. I think of seeing Mother and Father again and how they might have changed. And Tom. It's sure that he'll *be changed. And most of all I think will I ever return to Ireland? Will I ever see you all again? Will I ever have another friend like Julia?*

It's strange that when I'm talking to Ellie and the Ryans and all the other people here I don't think about all these things. Only when I'm alone in bed at night. I wish I could wake up tomorrow in my own bed in Shandon and hear the friendly bells that tell me all is well. Maybe I will again some day. Good night, dear, dear Uncle Charlie and Auntie Norah. God bless you.

Your loving niece, Annie

3

THE GOLDEN-DOLLAR GIRL

The voyage was to last another six days and the young Moores were glad they had found their sea legs, as the weather turned decidedly nasty again after St Stephen's Day and they were confined indoors for most of the day. The boys spent much of their time with John Ryan and a couple of the other married men who seemed happy to keep them amused playing cards, buckets and even shove-halfpenny on the long saloon tables while mothers tended babies and toddlers, some of whom were sick and miserable for the entire voyage.

Annie soon relaxed and stopped worrying about her two young brothers if they weren't at her side all the time. She trusted John Ryan as if she'd known him all her life. This allowed her to spend much of her time with Ellie and such is the nature of shipboard friendships, they soon knew as much about one another as if they were sisters. Mary Ryan joined in with them occasionally but rested a lot as she was expecting her first baby and was inclined towards anxiety.

'You'd think she was the first woman ever to have a

child,' sniffed Ellie, who came from a family of ten and didn't have any time for wishy-washiness, as she called it.

'Perhaps she's frightened that the baby will come before she gets to Minnesota,' said Annie out of pity for poor Mary, who had been sickly since they had left Queenstown.

Although all the women sharing their dormitory were English-speaking, Annie thrilled at the sound of the foreign tongues she heard around her on board, and the two girls soon vied with each other to distinguish one language from another.

'I learned French with the nuns but it doesn't sound a bit like that French family we met,' said Ellie.

'Never mind, Ellie,' Annie replied. 'We'll not need it at all when we arrive. 'Tis American we need to be learning.' She did her best imitation of an American accent, making Ellie collapse into giggles.

Annie's long dress, worn for the first time on Christmas Day, was now worn every evening at suppertime but try as she might, she couldn't manage to fix her hair in quite the same style as Ellie had done for her on Christmas Night and usually ended up shaking out her long auburn curls impatiently and leaving them loose over her shoulders.

'What a fine head of hair you have,' some of the women often remarked as they took turns brushing it for her at bedtime. 'It shines like copper,' said one.

Annie laughed. 'That's why they call me Copperknob,' she retorted.

Suspended in this unreal world at sea, Annie hardly

noticed the last six days of the journey passing and had quite got used to the discomforts of shipboard life. Around her she heard the older women talk incessantly about America – wondering what kind of conditions would they find there, would there be work, would people be kind, would they make good . . .

Finally, the day dawned when they received instruct-ions from the stewardess to start packing their belongings as they would be making their entrance to New York Harbour on the following morning. A palpable air of excitement suddenly pervaded the ship, and the pas-sengers, who until then had seemed quietly content with their lot, all at once seemed to become focused on what was ahead as if awaking from a dream.

'We'll arrive outside the harbour late tonight,' John Ryan informed the girls. 'Then first thing tomorrow, they'll send a ferry out for us – just like the tender at Queenstown – and that will bring us in to Ellis Island.'

Annie thought of her parents who would, no doubt, be as excited right now as she was, preparing to see their three children again after all this time. She busied herself packing and getting her worsted costume ready for the next day. She wanted to look her best for her family and toyed with the idea of wearing her hair up, but that, she thought, might be too much of a shock and they might not even recognise her. No, she'd save the long dress and the new grown-up hairstyle as a surprise. Tomorrow, she mused, as she gathered their belongings into some kind of order, would be the most exciting day of her life so far, and certainly the most eventful birthday.

That night, she and Ellie remained awake far into the

night, too excited to sleep, planning in whispers how they would write to each other and even, perhaps, visit with each other in the future.

'After all, it's all the same country, Ellie,' reasoned Annie. 'We're sure to see each other some time.'

They awoke to a new world. The sound of hooting and the unaccustomed stillness of the boat got them out of bed earlier than usual on that bitterly cold New Year's morning. An astounding sight met their eyes when they all hurried on deck before breakfast.

'Oh look, Ellie, look,' cried Annie. 'We've arrived at last!'

Seagulls wheeled around the mast. Where until then, they had lived in a world empty of anything but water, now they were faced with a vast panorama which made them gasp.

They had expected land to be visible as they knew they would have dropped anchor outside the harbour the night before. But the sight, not only of land but of the array of steamships, cargo vessels, passenger ferries and sailing craft all around them, took their breath away.

'Wait until I tell Uncle Charlie about all these ships,' exclaimed Anthony, wide-eyed. 'They're just capital, so they are.'

Then Annie saw it – rising triumphantly out of the early morning mist as if to salute them – the famous Statue of Liberty, the symbol of hope for so many just like her, come to the United States to start a new life. A lump rose in her throat as she thought of how Uncle Charlie would love to see this. He had talked so much about the 'green lady' as the statue was called: how it had been given to the Americans by the French only five years before; how it was three-hundred-and-five feet high and made of three hundred copper sheets joined together. He had even taught her the words engraved on the base of the statue, written by a lady called Emma Lazarus. Annie knew them off by heart.

Give me your tired, your poor, your huddled masses yearning to breathe free.

Annie whispered those words now in awe. Behind the statue, the city of New York loomed, and as the mist lifted, they beheld a vast spread of buildings as far as the eye could see. They gazed and gazed. Even the boys were struck silent, until little Philip queried in a small voice. 'How will we find Ma and Da, Annie?'

'Don't worry, Philip, they'll know where to find us,' Annie answered reassuringly, but her voice quavered with doubt.

The next few hours flew by. After eating as much as they could get hold of for breakfast – 'Eat up,' John Ryan had warned, 'you won't get anything again for hours.' – they had to get their baggage on deck ready for departure on the harbour ferry, which was to fetch them mid-morning and carry them into Ellis Island, the landing station.

There was particular excitement on this occasion, as the new immigrant landing station at Ellis Island was this very day open for the first time.

'The Commissioner of Immigration and all the government people will be there to greet us,' the stewardess announced in her usual bustling, self-important way. 'We might even be the first ferry to arrive in,' she added.

The little group was agog and everyone's eyes strained to be the first to catch sight of the harbour ferry coming out for them. All the passengers were now gathered together on each deck and for the first time since the day they had left Queenstown, Annie spied Mike Tierney, the kind young man who had helped her. What a long time ago that seemed now. He, of course, had been in the single men's quarters, so they were hardly likely to have met. She greeted him with enthusiasm and introduced him to Ellie and the Ryans. Mike was the first to spot the ferry coming towards them. The side-wheeler drew up alongside the *Nevada* and even though they were on the lowest of the four decks, they had to crane their necks to get a good view of the ferry below.

Bedecked with coloured bunting, it presented an exotic spectacle to the travel-worn and apprehensive passengers on board the *Nevada*.

'Look at that Annie, there's a lucky omen for you,' Mike Tierney pointed at the ferry. 'It's called the *John E. Moore*. How's that for a great start? You've only just arrived and they're calling the boats after you.'

Everyone who heard him laughed. Annie blushed with excitement and pleasure, and suddenly she was filled with hope once again. Of course her parents would find them. Weren't they expecting them this very day and wasn't it her fifteenth birthday for goodness sake? They would be out there waiting to welcome them already.

Annie and the boys were almost the last to board the ferry, first- and second-class passengers as usual getting priority, but finally they started to move towards the gangplank and once again Mike Tierney came to Annie's aid, swinging her small trunk up on his shoulder as if it was a feather's weight and carrying their rolled-up bedding under his free arm. At last the ferry gate clanged shut and the *John E. Moore* headed back to the shelter of the harbour with all one hundred-and-seven SS *Nevada* passengers safely on board. They passed three other large steamships near the mouth of the harbour, all waiting to land their passengers, but it now appeared they would indeed be the first arrivals.

As they neared the gigantic Statue of Liberty, Annie saw just how magnificent it really was, how proud was its stance as, one arm topped by a gold torch raised aloft in greeting, it seemed to welcome them into its world.

They were not long inside the harbour and heading towards the splendid four-towered building which housed the new landing station at Ellis Island when they became aware of the commotion and fanfare awaiting them. Bells were ringing, whistles sounded off and word spread on board the ferry that they were the first arrivals on this auspicious day. As they drew alongside the wharf, they beheld a huge crowd waiting and then the cheering started.

A burly German passenger stood beside Annie and the boys, almost blocking their view of this amazing spectacle. As the gangplank was run ashore, he made to step out on to it but a restraining hand was placed on his arm.

'Ladies first,' said Mike Tierney, and, taking hold of her trunk again, he nudged Annie forward onto the gangplank. Annie needed no second bidding and laughing, she tripped across it into her new life without a backward look. With the boys close behind her and the sound of cheering and clapping ringing in her ears, she took the stairs leading to the registration office two at a time and only hesitated when she reached the top and saw a row of very important-looking gentlemen waiting to greet her.

All the New York newspapers of the following day carried reports of what happened next. Annie Moore's fifteenth birthday became not only a day she would not easily forget but one which ensured her place in history.

First Immigrant On Ellis Island

Annie Moore Heads the Procession of Those Registered at the New Federal Depot

One of the happiest children in New York last night was Annie Moore, a pretty fifteen-year-old Irish girl, who with her two brothers, arrived on the Guion line steamship, *Nevada*, from Queenstown yesterday. For Annie was reserved the privilege of being the first steerage passenger to land at the new immigrant depot on Ellis Island.

Every preparation had been made to begin the work of landing immigrants at the new depot when the transfer steamer *John E. Moore* ran into the Ellis Island basin at 11 o'clock in the forenoon with the 107 immigrants from the *Nevada*. The big double doors leading to the main stairway near the centre of the building were open and at the head of the stairway stood Colonel Weber, Superintendent of Emigration, while near him was Mr Charles Hendley, who came all the way from Baltimore to register the first immigrant to land at the new depot.

'Here they come!' exclaimed one of the gatemen as a chorus of whistles from the steam vessels in the vicinity announced that the immigrants were landing. Three tremendous cheers went up from the employers and Colonel Weber was surprised to see a rosy-cheeked ... girl skipping up the stairs two steps at a time. She was at the head of the column and immediately behind her were her two brothers.

First To Land

When Annie saw the grave-looking gentleman waiting to receive her she hesitated for a moment, but the crowd behind pressed on, and before she knew it she was entering the big room north of the registry desks.

Treasurer Manning led her up to one of the desks, where Mr Hendley, pen in hand, was waiting.

'What is your name, my girl?' asked Mr Hendley.

'Annie Moore, Sir,' answered the girl. Annie was from County Cork and she was bound for her parents' home at No 32 Monroe Street, this city.

The ordeal of examination over, Annie and

her brothers passed down one of the aisles leading through the registry department to the room beyond, where Colonel Weber stood waiting with a ten dollar gold piece, which he presented to Annie, wishing her at the same time, a Happy New Year.

If she had been surprised at the attention shown her before she was now absolutely dumbfounded. She blushed and stammered and finally managed to ask:

'Is this for me to keep, Sir?'

She was assured that it was . . .

Annie was then hurried along to the local waiting room, where she found her parents, and in less than half an hour from the time she landed she was on her way to the city to spend the rest of New Year's Day.

New York Herald, 2 January 1892, p. 2.

Annie's head was spinning. She stood speechless, looking at the gleaming, solid gold piece filling the palm of her hand. The splendid-looking gentleman, wearing the widest, tallest hat she'd ever seen, had finished his speech and was smiling at her in a kindly way. All around her people were clapping and cheering.

Then she and the boys were escorted out of the big registration hall with the enormous arched windows and led downstairs towards the crowded waiting area and the spot later to become known as 'the kissing post', where passengers were reunited with family and friends.

The noise level increased as the trio approached the

barrier, and suddenly Annie saw him! There was her father, shouting and beckoning to her, his familiar, ruddy features expanded into an ear-to-ear smile of welcome. 'Father, Father, here we are,' she cried, running excitedly to throw herself into his arms. What a flood of relief and affection seized her. She clung to him as he swung her around in delight. The boys looked on in amazement, suddenly overcome by shyness towards this father they had not seen in three years.

'Mother!' cried Annie, 'where's Mother?' She turned around and there was Mother, arms held out, speechless with joy. They hugged and hugged, half-laughing, half-crying, and the boys soon joined in the mêlée as they recognised their long-lost parents. They were home at last.

4

A FEW SURPRISES

Much later, when Annie looked back on her first weeks in New York City, she realised that they had made a greater impact on her than anything else in her life before. Sometimes she thought that she was living a whole new life and had been reborn; at other times she considered her real life to have been what had gone before and felt a keen sense of loss as it gradually receded and became suffused in a rosy but faded memory like an old photograph.

She wrote home often – to her aunt and uncle as well as to Julia Donohue – copious letters full of details about her new life in New York.

The sights, the sounds, the smells that filled her nostrils as soon as she set foot on American soil were almost overwhelming. Once they had been deposited at Battery Park by the small ferry which plied between Manhattan and Ellis Island, they had to wait in the icy-cold wind while Father fetched a horse cab. As they stood there clutching their belongings, Annie's impression of New York was that it was a rough and dangerous place. She and the boys clung to their mother's side as vendors shouted their wares and grubby street urchins pestered the newly-arrived passengers for money.

Annie gazed out the cab window at the towering buildings they passed on the way to her new home in this extraordinary place. How would she ever get used to it? Her misgivings increased when they got to No 32 Monroe Street – not a great distance from Battery Park. It was a long street lined with tall dirty-looking tenement buildings which seemed to block out the sky. Up they struggled with their bags and bundles through a dark, narrow and malodorous stairwell. Smells of strange foods assailed them at each landing yet familiar sounds of family-life echoed behind each closed door. They encountered no one on their way up.

'Here we are,' Father announced cheerfully, as they reached a door on the third floor. He opened the door and led the way in. Annie's first impression was one of utter shock. The door opened onto a small cramped, dark apartment. There was only one window looking out on the street, and the whole dwelling seemed to consist of just three small rooms – the living-room-kitchen she found herself in and two windlowless rooms leading off it. It can't be true, she thought disbelievingly, how can we possibly all live here? At Uncle Charlie and Auntie Norah's she'd had a whole room to herself – a tiny box room granted, but all her own nonetheless.

This was nothing like what she had expected, not even close to the idea she'd had of a home in America. Not that she'd expected anything grand, but this – a poky, dark, little place you couldn't swing a cat in – she just couldn't believe it.

But then her eye was caught by a colourful banner stretched across the wall above the small stove. 'Happy Birthday Annie and Welcome Home To You All,' it read. She swallowed hard and looked at her beaming parents. She had seen the way they had bundled the baggage out of sight so as not to crowd the small room, the way the table was all set for a meal and the familiar mementoes from home in evidence everywhere, and she knew that she owed it to them to appear as pleased as they were. She bit her lip hard and tried to smile. 'Yes, here we are at last,' she said.

There were a lot more surprises in store for Annie, but having to put a brave face on her initial disappointment somehow armed her to deal a little better with what was ahead. Sharing a room with Philip and Anthony was the least of her problems, she reflected wryly. God knows, she had become quite used to that during the voyage across from Ireland when they had been packed so closely together in steerage.

Her older brother, Tom, who now seemed like a grown man to Annie, lodged with some of his workmates near the hotel where he worked in downtown Manhattan, and the family saw him only on his day off. However, he still contributed to the household, and Annie very quickly saw how essential his contribution was. She learned more about the realities of earning a living in America in that first week than she would have learned in five years back in Ireland. She was very soon stripped of all the illusions she had held that the streets of America were paved with gold. Not her street anyway. Gone was the hope that she could continue her education, and as for continuing her music lessons – that was out of the question.

'Grow up, girl, who do you think you are – a lady?' her father had snorted one night in the first harsh words spoken since their arrival. 'You'll have to bring in money. The boys too – I can get them some delivery work after school.'

They had been sitting around the table; it was nine o'clock at night a few days after their arrival and Matt Moore was not long returned from his work at the shirt factory. Mother was serving out mutton stew and the room was still full of lengths of material and sewing paraphernalia that she had been toiling over all day long.

It was obvious that they lived in an area which was as poverty-stricken as any the Moores had seen in Cork. But it seemed to Annie to be a different kind of poverty people suffered from here. It seemed to have more to do with overcrowding than lack of food. The great numbers of people everywhere was what struck her most at first. And it seemed everyone spoke different languages. Later she was to find this quite exhilarating – when she became less timid and more sure of her environment.

On the day after their arrival when Mother had brought them out to nearby Hester Street to do the marketing, Annie had been astounded, not only at the jostling crowds but at the babble of different languages and different kinds of people she saw all around her.

'There's all sorts living around here,' Mother told them. 'Germans, Italians, Polish and Russian Jews as well as Irish people like ourselves.'

Hester Street was obviously one of the main meeting points in the Lower East Side, as the district was called.

The street was lined with stalls and pushcarts with peddlers selling everything imaginable – foods Annie had never seen or even heard of as well as clothes and household goods. Stout barrels piled high with olives, nuts, pickles and fruits of all kinds stood sentry at each stall; strange, exotic aromas came from food stores where a variety of sausages such as the children had never seen hung from hooks along with salted meats and the counters groaned with cheeses, sauerkraut and pickles; and the fish stands, piled high with all manner of smoked, salted and fresh fish, were another revelation. Mother bought a pretzel for each of them from a kerbside stand as a treat and watched their expressions with amusement as they savoured these chewy morsels for the first time.

The pushcart peddlers – many of them bearded and wearing long coats, were a lively lot, crying out their wares with gusto as they hugged themselves to keep warm. One of them, his cart overflowing with women's dresses, shawls and bloomers, caught Annie's eye and beckoned to her, letting flow a torrent of words she didn't understand.

'He's speaking Yiddish,' explained Mother. 'He's trying to get you to buy something.'

Annie's puzzled look didn't put him off. Smiling even more, he switched into English. 'Hey, shiksa! How about a fine petticoat? Best bargain in town, you'll see,' he urged.

Smiling at Annie's confusion, Mother called out, 'Not today, thanks,' and they moved on.

The boys were enthralled by a blade-sharpener with a portable grinder, who tinkled a little bell for attention shouting, 'Scissors to grind, razors to grind . . . bring your penknives, carving knives, any old knives!'

A horse and cart would occasionally push its way through all the action to make a delivery, causing further uproar – drivers shouting warnings at the crowd, huge dray horses snorting loudly and swishing their tails as they drew to a reluctant halt under the lash of the whip. High above this hive of activity, lines of washing hung across some of the narrower side streets, suspended precariously between the buildings on flimsy clothes lines. Petticoats danced merrily in the bitter January breeze and Annie looked up in amazement, wondering how on earth their owners would ever retrieve them.

'Make haste, Annie, or we'll miss the best cuts of meat,' urged Mother, as she pushed through the crowds with the boys close on her heels.

The butcher, Mr Abraham – a huge, bearded man with a jolly face and a twinkle in his brown eyes – obviously knew Mother and hailed her like an old friend. 'Ah, at last the family have arrived Mrs M. Let me have a look. You one lucky woman now with three more mouths to feed. So, let me see, what a fine grown-up daughter, and a pretty one too, eh?' He beamed at Annie. 'And the sons too. We gotta get something really tasty today ain't that so. How about a fine bit of mutton . . . '

As he spoke he was choosing and cutting meat at great speed and within seconds he held it out to show Mother. Annie looked around her at the bustling throng. The buzz of activity reminded her of the Butter Market in Shandon, but that was where the resemblance ended.

'Annie, stop dreaming and give me a hand with these

groceries,' called Mother. 'I have little time to spend idling the morning away here. I have work to be getting on with.'

As they wound their way home again through the busy streets, Mother explained how she had to get a certain amount of sewing work done every day for Mr Jacobson from Smith & Dobson's; otherwise she wouldn't get paid enough. She sometimes even had to work on Sundays if there was a lot to be done or if Mr Jacobson was short one of his regular pieceworkers.

Before the week was out, a picture of what life in America would be like was gradually becoming clearer to Annie. She now saw her parents in a new light. She couldn't help but notice how much they had aged in the three years since she had last seen them. Her mother was thinner and more worn-looking and even her father – a naturally rumbustious figure – looked a little beaten. It was a hard struggle they'd had to get this far.

Privately, in her bed at night, as she listened to their quiet murmurings in the next room, Annie wondered what was the point of it all. Why come to America at all if you couldn't be better off than you'd been in Ireland? Yes, they'd been poor at home in County Cork, but at least they'd had friends and family around them; they'd had a bit more space and the beauty of the countryside – trees, grass and hedgerows – had been within easy reach.

This kind of thinking usually reduced Annie to tears of homesickness, but she made sure to pull the comforter right over her head for fear anyone would hear her.

In her letters home to Cork she wrote only in positive terms of her new life. She knew instinctively that she would be letting the side down if she were to reveal the truth about the reality of her parents' struggle. Instead she comforted herself by taking out the handsome little journal Julia had given her as a going-away present and confided her misgivings to it whenever she had an opportunity.

America's so much different than I thought it would be, she wrote late one night by the light of a peg lamp, long after the boys had fallen asleep.

Life is hard here. Mother and Father work so hard and the talk is all of making money. Mother says that life will improve if we all work hard to bring in more money and that in a year or two we should be able to get a better apartment, perhaps one with a parlour. It will all be worth it in the end, she says, as America is really the land of opportunity even if we can't see that yet.

I hope she's right as she and Father and Tom have already worked so hard for so long and they still have so little. When I say this, she becomes angry and says I've become spoilt living the easy life back home in Ireland. Two more years in this cramped, dark place – I hate to think of it!

We are on the third floor and all I can see when I look out are the windows of the houses opposite and the iron fire escapes that run down the outside of all the buildings. I hope we'll never have a fire to escape from. In winter you never see anyone on them, but Father says that when it becomes very hot in summer, people often sit out on them and some even bring out their mattresses and sleep there.

What fun that would be!

The El-train crosses high above our street on a huge iron bridge and all night long I can hear it roaring by or screeching to a halt. It makes a terrible noise – much louder than the Dublin Express coming into Glanmire. But I'm getting used to it. Just now I can hear the Walenski's baby crying.

The Walenskis are our Polish neighbours on the second floor and they have four children. Mrs Walenski is friendly and very kind to everyone. But the smells in the house are terrible – they cook very strange food. Not as strange as the Petrowskis next door though. What I would give for some grand Cork bacon and some butter from the market.

I like to get out and we had such fun on Father's day off last Sunday. He brought us walking in Central Park – a fine big park with a lake – and we watched the gentry driving there in their carriages and saw lots and lots of people skating on the lake. I would be frightened of falling through the ice but the boys are mad to try. It's bad enough trying to walk on the icy streets sometimes. I must tread very carefully or I'd get soaked. Twice I fell on the ice this week and once I thought I'd sprained my ankle but a kind gentleman helped me to my feet and after a moment or so I could put my foot to the ground and off I went. I'll have to be mindful of carriages and streetcars turning over too as the horses can also slip on icy streets.

I spend my days helping Mother with the sewing, but I don't get any pay for it. She only gets five cents an hour and she says I will have to find work and earn money myself. I don't think I could make much money at this work. As it is, I'm not good enough to use the machine, but I can sew on buttons and clip the threads along the seams.

The boys will be starting school next week with the nuns in the convent nearby. I could go into service with a family. They say many Irish girls my age do that but then I would have to leave home and live in with strangers. I'd like best if I could find some work and remain here with the family.

5

MAKING A LIVING

Annie's opportunity to earn her living came soon enough. Mrs Walenski called to their door one morning a couple of weeks after the children's arrival. She, like Annie's mother, worked at home, but Mrs Walenski took in ironing. A position was coming up shortly at the laundry she worked for, she told them, and if they liked she would mention Annie's name to her employer, Mr Rosen. 'A big, strong gal like you, it's okay, I think. What you say?'

Annie didn't hesitate a second and Mother looked pleased when she answered up boldly. 'Yes, I'd like to try, Mrs Walenski.'

Mrs Walenski was as good as her word and presented Annie to Mr Rosen on his next visit a couple of days later. He cast an approving look over the healthy, red-cheeked Irish girl and told her to come to the Phoenix Laundry to see his boss next morning at seven-thirty sharp.

Annie was up at the crack of dawn next morning and gratefully downed the bowl of oatmeal that Mother placed in front of her before heading out into the cold, frosty morning.

Although still pitch-dark, the streets were alive with people rushing to work, and she had to keep her wits about her to make sure she didn't lose her way. The route Father had outlined for her took thirty minutes to walk, and she arrived at the tall redbrick building in good time and stood aside at the door to let a flood of women pour through the doors and down the stairs.

Swallowing hard, she passed through the door and approached a stern-looking man sitting in a small glass-walled office near the entrance. 'I've come to see Mr Dunbar about a job. Mr Rosen said to come,' she added, seeing the man look at her doubtfully.

'Wait there,' he barked and turned to speak to an older man who had just entered the office.

They peered down at her through the glass partition and she was beckoned through the door. Then she was escorted along a dark passageway to Mr Dunbar's office and after waiting around a minute or two, a gruff voice called, 'Enter'.

'A young lady looking for work. Says you're expecting her,' her escort explained to the enormously fat, purple-faced man seated behind the desk.

'Name?' he asked, peering at her over steel-rimmed spectacles.

When she told him Mr Rosen had sent her, the man nodded briskly and asked her a long list of questions. What age she was, when she had come to America, where she lived, with whom, what was the state of her health ... Eventually, he seemed satisfied and instructed her to go downstairs and report to Mrs McCrudden in the ironing hall. She was to start right away.

She would be paid $3 a week as a 'folder' and would start work every morning at seven-thirty. The words shot out of his mouth like bullets out of a gun but Annie was thrilled and needed no second bidding.

'Thank you so much, Mr Dunbar. Thank you,' she stammered, not knowing whether to bow in the direction of this powerful personage or just to remove herself as fast as possible.

'Away with you,' thundered Mr Dunbar.

Annie had no need to ask the way. The hum of machinery, the clang of heavy vessels, the hiss of the steam irons, the sound of raised voices and the damp, steam-filled air all drifted up to meet her as she hurried down the dimly lit stairs. Her heart pounded when she found herself in a vast hall where white-clad women moved purposefully in every direction.

No need to ask who was in charge either. A tall, powerful-looking woman stood on a platform at one end of the hall. Her voice seemed to dominate everything and everyone as she directed proceedings in staccato tones.

This was the ironing hall, and strange-looking machines were lined along the walls. These, she was to find out, were called rotary irons and were heated by gas jets inside twin rollers. This was what made the air so hot and steamy. In front of each machine stood women on platforms, operating huge protruding pedals by stepping on them. At first glance it looked to Annie as if these women were engaged in a strange, slow, ghostly dance, suspended as they were above floor level and so intent on what they were doing.

In the centre of the room stood rows of long wooden

trestle tables where more women were working. They were busy folding articles which they then placed in baskets beside them. Nobody seemed to notice Annie and she crept slowly along one side until she came level with the platform. Her voice, when she spoke sounded like a squeak to her own ears.

'Are you ... are you Mrs McCrudden?' she ventured, swallowing hard as the gimlet eyes focused on her at last. Receiving no answer, just a piercing stare, she added quickly, 'Mr Dunbar sent me. I'm the new folder.'

Mrs McCrudden nodded, motioned to an alert-looking girl standing at the head of one of the tables. 'Take her, Alice. Fit her out and put her on Table Four.'

That was it. She didn't even ask my name, thought Annie, as she moved hurriedly after Alice, who flashed her a quick smile. Within minutes, Alice had taken her to a cloakroom where the women kept their outdoor clothes and other belongings, and handed her a huge white apron which when secured with long ties covered her from neck to toe.

'Tie up those tresses or Mrs Mac will get mad,' hissed Alice, throwing Annie a large white kerchief which managed to cover all of her hair and tie neatly at the back of her neck. Then she whisked Annie through the door in front of her and propelled her across to a table near the front of the room right under the eyes of Mrs Mac. Without further ado, Annie was handed a basket full of garments and told to fold them exactly like the girl next to her.

'You have to work fast,' muttered Alice before she returned to her own place. There was no talking permitted but the other women and girls at the table gave her a brief look and some smiled guardedly without stopping what they were doing. Up and down the room roamed the same older man Annie had seen upstairs at the front door. He, she was to find out later, was the supervisor, Mr Gibson, and you disobeyed him at your peril.

The rest of the day passed in a blur and so tired was she at the end of it that when she stumbled out onto the street at eight o'clock that evening, it took her some minutes to get her bearings and realise that she was not on the streets of Cork but right at the centre of New York. She headed home, glad to be out in the fresh air, no matter how cold it was. Her back and shoulders were aching and it was a relief to walk. There were still people hurrying along the dark streets, returning from work like herself, and it struck her for the first time that she would not be seeing daylight for some time to come.

As that rather unpleasant thought registered, she felt a tremor of apprehension pass through her and a feeling of being trapped, of there being no going back now. She seemed for a moment to lose her individuality and to have joined a human river of people, all flowing in the same direction, one inseparable from the other. Then she shook herself and shrugged off such fanciful notions. 'I can always go back to Ireland,' she murmured sleepily to herself as she trudged homewards, and the thought comforted her mightily.

In the weeks ahead Annie came to look forward to the walk to and from work when she could sort out all the new impressions and experiences that had taken over her life. Keeping a journal was a luxury she could no longer afford. Once she arrived at the laundry it took all her concentration to manage to stay on her feet working all day long, and when she finally reached home in the evenings, all she could do was eat the food Mother set in front of her before falling on to her bed to sleep.

As she walked along the busy streets, she daydreamed about home. She wondered what Julia would be doing now. She thought too of Ellie King and what kind of life she had made for herself in Nebraska. She wished they could meet again. She thought occasionally of Mike Tierney, the young tailor she'd met on board the steamer. He worked in New York. But looking around her at the crowds of people coming and going she knew it would be nothing short of a miracle if she ever bumped into him. Anyway, she thought, the life of a tailor must be very different to her own or that of her family.

She marvelled at this great metropolis which throbbed with life no matter what the hour. She had now become quite accustomed to the El, which exploded across her line of vision every so often like the fireworks she'd heard you could see at Coney Island in the summertime. But she still gazed in awe at some of the really high buildings reaching proudly for the sky – and all lit up they were at night. The highest one of all – the New York World Building – was twenty-two storeys high, according to Tom, and was known as a 'skyscraper'. It had been opened only the year before, but he reckoned that many more would be built now and he was thinking strongly of going into the building trade himself, as there would always be work and they said you could make a lot of money at it.

She was fascinated too by the street hawkers, selling

everything from oysters and hot corn to gloves and suspenders. And they weren't all boys like the newsboys at home in Cork. All the corn sellers were girls and they weren't a bit timid, shouting out their wares bravely, 'Hot corn! Hot corn! Piping hot! Oh what beauties I have got!'

She'd treated herself to some the night she'd received her first pay packet, thrilled to be able to buy something with her own money. She'd have sooner gone without, though, after the scolding she'd had from Father for not bringing all her money home. She'd been really resentful as she felt she deserved to keep some of it. But Father thought otherwise.

'How do you think we're going to feed ye all if you go spending good money on whatever catches your fancy,' he'd asked angrily. He became even angrier when she'd answered him back. 'Listen girl, you obey the rules here or you'll find yourself out looking for someone else to feed and clothe you.'

Annie still simmered with annoyance over it, and she determined to find some way of saving a little money for herself. She began to long for a little independence and the freedom to shape her own life. Father had really changed, she thought, watching my every move and treating me like a child. Can't he see I'm grown up now? A couple of days later, however, all such petty resentments were forgotten in the face of a very real worry.

Annie returned home one evening to find knots of people standing out on the doorsteps and the sidewalks – notwithstanding the bitter cold – talking in hushed tones. Mother beckoned to her.

'What's happened, Mother? Has there been an accident?'

'It's the typhus,' Mother replied gravely. 'They have it next door in No 31. Mr Abramowitz had to be taken away to hospital today. They've been fumigating the house all day. And the inspectors have been in all the houses around – ours too – to see if there are any more cases. They've also found cases of it in No 85. We'll have to be very careful and pray to the dear Lord it doesn't strike us.'

Later they heard that Mr Abramowitz had not long arrived from Russia and was thought to have contracted typhus on the ship.

'Zose inspectors are no good,' Mrs Petrowski confided to Mother. 'Zey see dis man at Ellis Island and zey don't see he is too seeck to come to America. And zey try to stop me because I have a leetle cough. Pshaw!' Mrs Petrowski snorted disgustedly.

A few days later they heard that Mr Abramowitz had died in Bellevue Hospital. That week two nurses from the hospital called to all the houses in the neighbourhood and spoke to people about how to stay healthy and avoid catching the deadly disease. The authorities now feared an epidemic and there were reports about it every day in the newspapers. So far there were seventy-four cases of typhus in New York City, Annie read, and they were nearly all around their neighbourhood.

Father said that whole families suspected of having the disease had been sent away to North Island, a quarantine centre outside Manhattan. If that happened, he warned, you'd lose your job and maybe even your home and they wouldn't let you out of it for months.

6

A Fresh Perspective

At the laundry Annie's day was long and arduous, but she soon got to know most of the people who worked in the ironing hall and even some of the women who toiled over the huge vats next door in the wash room. They all stopped work every day at noon for a short dinner break, and this was Annie's opportunity to make new acquaintances and get a glimpse of the lives of her workmates.

There was Sophia Rostov, a girl of Russian background, about her own age, with long, dark shiny hair and black eyes. Annie thought she'd never seen anyone quite so pretty. Sophia was fun too, and she and Annie took to each other immediately and soon became fast friends. Then there was Alice Rodgers, the girl who'd taken charge of her on that first morning. All the workers looked up to Alice, who was about twenty and smart as they come. She had been working in the laundry a few years now and, though she had no time for any slacking, she was very fair and did her best to protect them all from the lash of Mrs McCrudden's tongue.

One afternoon, some weeks after Annie had come to

work at the laundry, they were all suddenly startled out of their monotonous routine by a fearful commotion next door in the wash room. The sound of a woman screaming rose above the din and suddenly bells started to ring and people began running in every direction. Mrs McCrudden made a run for the wash room, and Mr Gibson took the stairs two at a time to fetch help.

'What can have happened?' Annie asked the woman next to her. It was Kitty Mulhall, an older Irish woman who had been working in the laundry a few years.

''Tis sure someone's got scalded be the water or somethin' of that nature. It's happened before and God knows, 'twill happen agin.' Kitty shook her head resignedly, like one who'd seen it all before.

'A woman died in there two years ago,' recalled another woman. 'A vat of boiling water fell down on her when she was trying to move it. She was trapped and they couldn't get her out for a long while. She died later in the hospital.'

Some of the other women then began to recall accidents that had befallen people in the laundry, some in the ironing hall where it was very easy for the rotary iron workers to fall off the platforms or get their feet caught in the machinery.

'Them machines can be the devil all right,' said Kitty. 'You can catch your foot in them and get your leg mangled like poor Mary Ann Smith did two year ago. She had to have her leg amputated above the knee for a finish.'

'Is that really true?' asked Annie, sick with fear.

Seeing the panic on the younger girl's face, Alice tried to reassure her, but at that moment the screaming grew louder as the victim was borne swiftly past them on a stretcher and up the stairs and out of the building. They all stood in shock until Alice urged them back to work.

'There's nothing we can do right now,' she said in her calm voice. 'We'll hear what happened soon enough.' And indeed they hadn't long to wait before finding out that poor Becky Taylor was the unfortunate victim of a horrible scalding. She had leaned right over one of the huge vats of hot water to retrieve a garment that had got caught, but she slipped and her entire right side was scalded from wrist to shoulder. Even worse was to think that Becky was pregnant with her first child.

'At least the hospital is next door and they hadn't far to bring her,' said Annie, as she recounted the sorry tale to her parents when she got home later that night.

Mary Moore sighed and shook her head and for the umpteenth time wished the poor child didn't have to work such long hard hours at the laundry. God knows she was only fifteen. So much for the sixty-hours-a-week law. It was certainly not in force at the laundry, where Annie worked more than twelve hours a day most days of the week. Only on Saturdays could she get home in time for supper.

'At her age, I was running free although I did my fair share of work on the farm,' she said to Matt later in bed

She determined more than ever that she would do all in her power to get her friend Sister Bonaventure in St Ann's Convent nearby to use her connections to place Annie in domestic service. Sister Bonaventure was from Cork too and though she'd been ten years in America, she loved nothing better than to talk about the old country and exchange scraps of news with Mary over a cup of tea.

'It would be easier on the poor child, Matt,' said Mary, 'she'd live in a grand home and learn the ways of the gentry, and besides,' she added ruefully, 'she'd be living in and it would be one less mouth to feed.'

'Wisha and you know our Annie, she'd no sooner be living with the gentry than she'd be thinkin' she was one of them herself,' chuckled Matt, as he rolled over and went to sleep.

Worse was to come. Word got around the laundry in the following days that Becky Taylor had miscarried, and the injury to her arm was such that she would probably never work again. Many of the women muttered angrily about it.

'That's the last anyone will hear of that,' said one bitterly. 'She won't get a cent from Dunbar, that's for sure.'

'If an inspector came in here, he'd soon see how they treated us,' said one of the rotary operators. 'If we were men there'd be a union in here and then they'd have to compensate her.'

'Ssh,' warned Alice, 'do you want to get us all fired?'

It was dinner hour on the Monday of the week after the accident, and the women's anger and concern over their workmate's fate was spilling over like a boiling pot. Alice was surrounded by an angry group. Privately, she thought the women were right to be frustrated at their work conditions, but she also knew that if she didn't calm the firebrands among them there would be real unrest and that could only lead to job losses. She had seen it happen many times – those who spoke out were fired instantly if overheard by any of the senior staff, and there were always plenty of women waiting to take their place. Many times over the years the women had requested changes and safeguards to be put in place, but no improvements were ever made. Some of the machinery was badly out-dated, and Alice knew that accidents of a serious nature were only waiting to happen at the laundry.

This unhappy incident awakened Annie to the pitfalls of working at the laundry, and she resolved to find a different way of earning a living before too long.

Sophia felt the same way. 'I want to become a nurse,' she confided. 'But my brother's studies are going to cost a lot so my parents need me to earn money to help pay for his books. But I'm sure I would make much better money nursing once I was trained.'

Looking at Sophia, Annie thought she would make an excellent nurse. She had such a soft, sympathetic ex-pression, yet she was practical and strong too. Why should her brother be helped to do as he wished and not Sophia? It wasn't fair.

The Rostovs lived in Orchard Street, not very far from the Moores, much to Annie's delight. Sophia and Annie were drawn closer together since the accident at work and found they'd lots to talk about. Sophia revealed that there had been reports of typhus cases in her street too, 'and in Delancey Street where Papa's shop is,' she added, looking worried. 'They're also Russians. Papa knows one of the families.' She explained to Annie that there was a famine in Russia at the moment and that was why there were so many refugees crowding onto the ships to come to America, where they hoped to find a better life.

'But now they're here in America and fall ill with

typhus. It's so sad.'

'Will they die?' asked Annie.

'Many of them will,' replied Sophia. 'You see they are not very healthy to begin with. They are leaving Russia because they have not been able to survive there. Some of them arrive half-starving, Papa says.'

'It sounds like the Irish who came here after our Famine,' remarked Annie.

Sophia's family had been in America for five years now. Her father owned a junk shop on Delancey Street and she claimed you could buy just about anything in it. The peddlers brought in new things all the time, so you'd never know what you'd find from week to week. Sophia had two brothers, one older and one younger, she told Annie. In turn, Annie told Sophia all about her life in Cork, her journey to America and her reunion with her parents.

'You must meet my family soon,' urged Sophia. 'They would like you to visit, I know. And my Papa might let us come and help him in the shop some time.'

Sophia was as good as her word and one Saturday afternoon, Annie went home with her after work. It was the Sabbath, Sophia explained, and all the family would be at home.

'It's just like your Sunday. You go to church. We go to the synagogue,' explained Sophia, smiling.

The Rostov family lived in a building just like the Moore's, but the Rostov's was a much larger apartment and took up the top floor of the house at 29 Orchard Street. They climbed four flights of a dark, musty-scented staircase much like the one in Monroe Street, but when the door opened into the Rostov's apartment Annie found herself entering a new world. Delicious food smells wafted from beyond the cosy but ornately decorated living-room where the family was gathered.

No lamps were lit – only candles were permitted on the Sabbath – and the tall, highly-polished brass candlebra, standing in the centre of a table covered by a snowy-white lace tablecloth, shone in the candlelight.

'Hello, everyone. This is my friend Annie,' announced Sophia, propelling Annie into the room. Annie, suddenly overcome with shyness, could barely respond to the flood of warm greetings she received from Sophia's family. She was introduced to them all and soon relaxed in the company of these warm, friendly people.

Sophia's grandmama was a white-haired neat-looking old lady who sat in an armchair by the stove. Papa had a long, dark, curly beard like many of the men she had seen in the neighbourhood, and he gave Annie a hearty greeting from behind the dark head of the little boy who sat on his lap and to whom he was reading a story. Then there was Sophia's Mama whose hair – swept up in an elegant chignon – was exactly the colour of Sophia's, as were her eyes, which formed the same sickle-moon shape as Sophia's when she smiled.

'You're very welcome, Annie,' she said, sitting Annie down on a sofa near the window. A serious-looking young man seated at a desk in the corner looked up from his books and glanced shyly at Annie through his spectacles. Like his father and younger brother, he wore a little circular cap on the crown of his head. The yarmulka, as Annie was soon to find out, was worn by all Jewish males on the Sabbath and on other occasions.

'This is Josef,' Sophia told her, 'and he's studying very hard because he's going to be a rabbi one day.'

'Sophia tells us you've just come to America. Is it all very strange to you?' Papa asked.

'Yes, Annie, over supper you must tell us all about your country,' said Sophia's Mama.

Then it was all action as the table was laid and Mrs Rostov bustled in and out of the kitchen with the food.

'Annie, you may pull the chairs up and put the napkins at each place,' called Sophia.

Annie, ravenous at the appetising aromas coming from the kitchen, jumped up immediately to help. They all gathered around but before they sat down, Papa Rostov held his hands out over the table and said a prayer in Hebrew over the loaves of dark pumpernickel bread; he then raised a glass of wine aloft, said another short prayer in thanksgiving for the Sabbath and took a sip, passing the glass around for the others to sip from. After slicing the bread, he handed a piece to everyone around the table. Now the meal could begin.

Annie would never forget this first meal she shared with the Rostovs. She would always remember the family standing around the table with bowed heads in the flickering candlelight as their father blessed the bread, the exotic sound of the Hebrew words seeming to cast a magic spell on the proceedings.

The prayerful docility shown at the beginning of the meal was soon abandoned, and lively exchanges took place as Papa teased them all. Annie soon felt at ease – this was by far the most fun she'd had since she had come to America.

After supper they all took turns singing while Mrs Rostov accompanied them on the violin. When it came to Annie's turn she readily sang her old favourite – 'Believe Me If All Those Endearing Young Charms' – and received an enthusiastic response.

'What a fine voice you have, Annie,' exclaimed Mrs Rostov while Sophia cheered, pleased with the impression her new friend was making on the family. Even the studious Josef seemed impressed. He had removed his spectacles and Annie noticed that he too had those large, dark, luminous eyes.

'You must come and sing for us again,' he said, looking at her with new admiration. Annie, suddenly self-conscious, blushed to the roots of her hair.

'I must be getting along home now,' she announced. 'My parents will be anxious.'

'Papa and Josef will be with you some of the way,' said Mama Rostov, helping Annie with her coat and hat. 'They must be off to the synagogue shortly.'

Annie set off home between the two men, who accompanied her as far as Canal Street before turning off in the opposite direction towards the synagogue in Eldridge Street. They both shook hands with her formally on the street corner under the gas lamp, very sober-looking figures suddenly in their long dark coats and black hard hats.

'Please come and see us again soon,' said Mr Rostov. 'We enjoyed your visit very much.'

'Thank you, Sir, I had a very nice time,' replied Annie, suddenly feeling overcome once more with shyness.

But as she hurried home through the dark streets, she

savoured the memories of the unusual and stimulating evening she had just spent with Sophia's family. How different their home was, not only from her own family's apartment nearby but from any home she had ever been in before. She experienced a sudden urge to taste as much of life as possible and to open herself to as many different influences as she possibly could.

'I think I am going to have a good life here in America after all,' she murmured as she tripped up the stairs of 32 Monroe Street.

Annie's visit to the Rostov family marked the turning point in her adjustment to her new life. It began to dawn on her that New York was full of people she could make friends with, and with this realisation, the feelings of fear, isolation and loneliness which had plagued her since she had arrived disappeared at last. In their place a new confidence grew, and she began to look around her with a fresh zest and curiosity she had not felt before.

Things had improved too between Annie and Father since those tense days the previous January when she had first arrived and had experienced such problems adjusting to her new home. Annie knew now that Father had felt bad about not letting her continue her education, but she also knew that he really had no other choice. He'd said as much a couple of months back when she'd been off sick with bronchitis for two days after completing three consecutive weeks' overtime.

'I know it's hard for you, Annie,' Father had said. 'You've done very well, lass. I don't like to see you doing too much overtime but I know too that beggars can't be choosers. Now I can't see my way to letting you take up your schooling again at the moment but there's no reason why we couldn't be putting a little money aside against the future. So how about you keep the overtime money aside for yourself and maybe if you save hard it will come in handy for bettering yourself.'

Annie was touched. Indeed she would save hard – but her biggest goal now would be her independence. Her dreams of betterment were no longer confined to education. She longed to travel and see more of this huge country; to learn more about all the very different kinds of people in it. That was one of the things she loved about America. People had come here from every country in the world to make a new life. No wonder it was called the New World. It was so different from Cork where you'd never see a black person or a Chinaman. You only read about them in books.

But America could be hard on people too. Annie had already glimpsed the misfortune which could overtake some in this great modern society. At the laundry she both met and heard about women in all sorts of predicaments. More often than not they were her own countrywomen.

Annie would not easily forget that night in February she had gone home from work with poor Kitty Mulhall, who had been taken ill at work. Kitty had five children, all under ten years of age. The family lived in the basement of a tenement house down near the East River where a lot of the immigrant Irish lived. They had to cross the railway tracks to get to it and then enter a very narrow alleyway before emerging into a dark, smelly courtyard. A low doorway just below the level of the yard led into

Kitty's home. Inside, all was dark and dingy. Two small children were asleep on a rickety old bedstead, curled up together like puppies, and a little girl of about eight was trying to relight the stove which had gone out.

'Where's your father?' was all Kitty said to the little mite.

'He went out a while back,' she replied, glancing furtively at Annie. Kitty muttered something that Annie couldn't quite hear, but she could tell Kitty was displeased and ashamed. She looked really ill and Annie wondered should she fetch help.

'No child, it will pass. It often happens. Just give me a hand to get this stove lit and you can be on your way.'

Two small boys, of about nine and ten years of age appeared in the doorway within minutes of their arrival. Between them they lugged in a box of coal. In no time at all they had the stove lit and a kettle on the hob. These were Kitty's sons.

'Please get into bed, Kitty, I can make something to eat,' Annie implored. Kitty needed no second bidding. Annie followed her into the back room which was in an even worse state than the kitchen and helped lower her onto a shaky, grimy bedstead covered with a dishevelled heap of sacking. All Annie could find in the way of food was a stale loaf and a pot of half-cooked beans on the stove. With the help of the older girl, she got everyone fed and then helped Kitty swallow a hot drink comprising a drop of whiskey – which she found on a shelf over the stove – mixed with hot water and a spoon of sugar. Then she organised the little ones into bed, talking softly and reassuringly to them all the while. They were all very timid and just looked up at her shiftily as if they too were ashamed of the way she had found them.

By the time Annie got away home herself it was near to midnight and there was still no sign of their father returning. She hurried along the ill-lit, empty alleyways, partly relieved to be out of such a terrible place and partly fretting that her parents would be really worried about her. How she pitied poor Kitty. She had already heard at work that Kitty's husband, Seamus, drank a lot more than was good for him and that it was up to Kitty to earn the money. How oh how did they manage at all? And Kitty's story was not unique. Annie had heard its like many times. She began to see her own home in Monroe Street as privileged. Humble it might be but it was a home – a place of order, rest and consolation.

7

CONEY ISLAND

New York was a different place entirely since spring had arrived suddenly in the middle of April, Annie wrote her Aunt Norah. It was no longer a punishment to be setting out so early in the morning. It was wonderful to be coming and going from work in daylight and everybody seemed more alive. Suddenly everything delighted Annie, from the flowering blossoms on the trees on Park Avenue to the fine ladies in their spring gowns and matching parasols. She felt she was seeing so much of her surroundings for the first time. She felt stronger now too than she'd felt during winter when she'd suffered badly with bronchitis. But now if she set out home in the evenings in damp clothes it was no matter. The balmy breeze dried them out in no time and she never got chilled. Even Monroe Street had taken on a new lustre. She looked forward to her first summer in New York.

'For all that they tell me in work that it's terrible in summer with the heat and the lack of air in the place,' she wrote.

Occasionally, of a Sunday, Sophia would bring Annie

in to her Papa's junk shop which, although closed on Saturdays for the Sabbath, was open on Sunday afternoons. He always gave them a warm welcome, making them sit beside the stove while he poured them tea from the samovar permanently sitting on top of it. Then he would offer them sweet iced cookies from a jar on the shelf behind his desk. Suitably nourished and warmed up the girls would then wander around the shop examining the items on sale. Annie marvelled at the variety of objects crammed into every corner of the shop, from shelves of old books and periodicals to household items that she had never seen before.

Sometimes Sophia's brother Josef was there, but invariably he had his nose buried in some book or other. He seemed very distant to Annie but one day she decided that he was just shy, and when she approached him to ask what he was reading she was rewarded with a warm smile which lit up his whole face.

'Longfellow,' he replied. 'Henry Wadsworth Longfellow. He's my favourite poet. Do you like him?'

'I don't know anything about him. Is he American?' asked Annie.

Josef immediately lost his shy manner and moved over on the window seat he occupied to make room for Annie. 'Yes, he was. He died ten years ago. He was a teacher but he gave it up to become a poet and became very famous. Listen to this,' he said.

> Often I think of the beautiful town
> That is seated by the sea;
> Often in thoughts go up and down
> The pleasant streets of that dear old town
> And my youth comes back to me.
> And a verse of Lapland song
> Is haunting my memory still;
> A boy's will is the wind's will
> And the thoughts of youth are long, long
>   thoughts.

'That's beautiful,' Annie responded dreamily, thinking nostalgically of Cork. 'Will you write like that one day?'

'How did you guess I wanted to?' Josef looked amazed.

'It wasn't too difficult now,' she replied, laughing. 'You don't see or hear anything else when you're reading those books. You look as if you are in another world altogether.'

Now every time she met Josef in the shop they talked together and he showed her a different poem. Annie grew to enjoy poetry, and her first purchase from Mr Rostov's shop was a little volume of poems by Emily Dickinson which he let her have cheap. Josef had helped her choose it. He told Annie that the writer was a recluse who spent her life hidden away from the world writing her poetry. Annie was fascinated. 'Just like the nuns at home,' she told Josef. She found many of the poems difficult to understand, but one or two sounded so good when she read them aloud to herself that understanding them didn't seem to matter.

'Josef must be fond of you, he talks so much to you. He never even shows his silly poetry books to anyone else,' teased Sophia, smiling at her friend's sudden blush of embarassment.

Sophia in turn had visited the Moores in Monroe Street and delighted them all with her charming ways. It turned out that Mother had often been a visitor to Papa Rostov's junk shop in Delancey Street. Indeed she had bought the family's one good oil lamp there as well as a couple of other small items.

'Papa will be pleased to know that,' said Sophia, smiling at such a happy coincidence.

Mother was pleased too. She had always liked the shop and Mr Rostov too, as he was not pushy like some of the other shopkeepers in the area, always chivvying you to buy their goods and hurrying to your side the moment you entered the premises. No, Sophia's Papa was always busy in the back of the shop or sometimes in winter he was sitting in an old spindle-backed rocking chair beside a toasty warm stove and looked quite indifferent as to whether you bought something or not.

Central Park was a favourite venue among the Moores. In winter they had seen the gentry ice-skating on the lakes of the park, the elegant women in their stylish costumes and fur muffs; or the fashionable parades of horse-drawn sleighs on the West Drive. Now that the warmer weather had arrived they went to Riverside Drive to watch the cyclists on their large one-, two- and three-wheeled machines. The bicycles for one person looked very tricky to the children and they couldn't understand for the life of them how the wheelmen, as they were called, could balance such machines.

But without doubt the best Sunday of that entire

summer was the day of the family excursion to Coney Island. This was a trip that had been planned for some time. It took place in early June when the temperatures were just beginning to rise to heights Annie and the boys found nearly unbearable compared to what they had been accustomed to in Ireland. It was no hardship then to leave the oppressive atmosphere of the tenement in Monroe Street and set out in the relative cool of the early morning. Mother had packed mounds of bread-and-butter sandwiches and hard-boiled eggs to eat, as well as a large bottle of sweet soda, knowing that appetites would be sharp at the seaside. They packed swimming costumes too and stickball to play on the beach, as well as spades to dig for clams.

The family set off on foot for the excursion steamer on the East River docks where they were to meet Tom. This was great news to Annie, who hardly ever saw her older brother as they were rarely off work on the same day.

'There's Tom, there's Tom,' Anthony sped ahead as they neared the dock where they were to embark. And there he was right enough, their tall, good-looking brother, eagerly awaiting them at the entrance to the wharf. He wrestled Anthony playfully, and after hugging Annie and his parents, swung a delighted Philip up on his shoulders.

'Follow me,' he called to them, threading his way expertly through the crowds to get to the ticket office.

'What fun this is going to be,' Annie laughed, looking with amazement at the cheerful throng of New Yorkers waiting to board the side-wheel steamboats lined along the quayside. Early as it was, the scene was one of hectic

holiday activity. Even the steamers had a festive appear-
ance, bedecked with coloured flags and sun canopies.
They looked forward to their trip up-river via the popular
resorts of Long Branch, Rockaway, Brighton Beach and
finally Coney Island.

'Stand in line here for the iron steamboat, the only all-
water route to Coney Island! Stand in line now, please!'

Having paid out their 50 cents each, the Moores stood
in line to board the steamer. Out on the river, the air
cooled by a refreshing breeze, Annie recalled her arrival
in New York Harbour just six months previously. She
looked around, at her father and brothers leaning over
the rails – father pointing out various landmarks – at her
mother sitting opposite her, eyes closed, holding her face
up to the warm sun, and marvelled at how much life had
changed for her in such a short time. Now they were all
here together. For so long they had been separated. Tom
caught her eye and smiling, came over to join her.

'Well, howdee Sis.' Tom had quite a pronounced
Yankee twang to his accent by now which amused Annie,
although she suspected it wasn't entirely natural. He was
a bit of a dandy, Tom, and at eighteen was already cutting
quite a dash with the ladies, she heard. But she was proud
of this handsome older brother and longed to see more
of him. There was always plenty of fun when Tom was
around.

'You look very fine today, Tom,' remarked Annie,
admiring the tall, fit-looking figure in knee breeches and
spats with a fine brown jacket and fresh boiled shirt. She
wondered how he could afford such style.

'I have to look fine, Sis. I might cut a shine with a girl

any moment. Anyways, how are ya? I hear you're making your fortune down at that laundry, washing sheets and the like.'

'I don't wash, Tom. I'm a folder. And there's no fortune. I must get a better position. Would you know of some job I could do in the hotel?'

'Sis, I've told you before, I wouldn't be in the way of getting you any job. I have trouble enough holding on to my own. Ain't you happy then?'

'It's very hard work, Tom. I hope not to have to work another winter there. I'm looking to do something which will leave me free for a couple of night classes,' Annie replied. 'As it is, I work most nights and get ill-paid for it.'

'The thing for you to do then Annie is to go into service with a fancy up-town family who'd give you a few evenings off. I've a pal whose sister's in service with the Eastman's on Park Avenue. She's got a right good life, I'm tellin' ya. I'll ask him about it and let you know what I can.'

'Thanks, Tom.' Maybe he was right, Annie reflected, thinking how Tom always made everything sound so easy and uncomplicated. Maybe it really was all that simple. She decided to abandon any thoughts of work and hardship and enjoy this great outing. And indeed the day that followed put all worries of that sort out of Annie's head.

They all agreed that bathing in those inviting waves should come first. That would cool them down before a picnic on the beach. Outside the City Bath Houses, they divided up the swimming costumes and Mother and Annie headed for the women's lockers and Father and the boys to the men's.

Well-accustomed to swimming at Crosshaven, the younger boys were anxious to show their father how accomplished they were and scampered off down to the water's edge as soon as they were ready. Tom too was fond of the water. He raced the boys down and dived headlong into the waves.

Annie was more inclined to dip her toe in daintily, reluctant to get her swimming suit drenched, until Tom came along and splashed her unmercifully so she gave in and joined in the fun. Mother stayed behind, promising to have the food ready on their return.

After lunch, Annie and Tom set off exploring, agreeing that they would be back in time to help pack up and go visit the fairgrounds.

'I'm going to show you the best sight, Sis,' Tom promised, as they walked along the promenade running parallel to the surf. This mile-and-a-half of wide paved avenue was a sight in itself, thought Annie, as she watched the handsome carriages coming and going and the stylish pavilions lining it, backs to the beach. There were all sorts of amusements and novelties to be seen, and Tom bought some salt water taffy from a booth for them to eat as they strolled along.

Tom's surprise was the Observatory, and indeed he fulfilled his promise when, huffing and puffing, they reached the top and looked at the splendid view along the beaches of Coney Island. From this distance the people strolling the promenade below looked like tiny armies of ants.

'This is a fine place to be, Tom,' cried a delighted Annie, who had never been up so high in her life.

'I knew you'd like it, Annie,' said Tom. 'Father brought

me here when I first came over to America. I thought then that if I tried very hard, I could see the old country,' he laughed.

'Will we ever see it again, Tom, I wonder,' Annie was a bit wistful. She was still prone to the occasional bout of homesickness. 'How Uncle Charlie would love this. He'd want to count every step to the top and measure how far we could see, I'll warrant.'

'Sure we'll see Ireland again, Sis,' Tom hugged her warmly.

There was a soft side to him, Annie realised, as he assured her that Uncle Charlie would certainly be here with them some day to enjoy the sights as indeed, he added, they would be back to visit Ireland one day.

'We'll be fine rich Yankees when we return, Annie, and they'll have to bow down to us when we step down from our carriages.'

Annie laughed uproariously at the idea of this and cheered up. Tom was a tonic. However, as they were walking back towards the beach he suddenly said something which took her aback.

'Have you still got your golden eagle, Annie?'

'I have, Tom. Why?

'You know, if you gave it to me I could make some more money on it for you and in no time you'd really be rich.'

'How could that be, Tom?' Annie felt uncomfortable suddenly.

'Well I know some folk who could get you a swell return on that money if they were to invest it.' Tom lowered his voice confidentially.

'But it's a special gold dollar piece, Tom, don't you see. It was given to me because I was the very first passenger to land at Ellis Island. I want to keep it until I'm old and maybe . . . oh, I don't know . . .maybe give it to my grand-children. I don't think of it as money, really, but as a kind of treasure.'

Annie was finding it difficult to explain this to Tom – who had turned very quiet suddenly.

'You know, Sis, we all need money in this family and don't you think it a fine thing that you would be able to be of help?'

'I don't think it could make that much difference, could it?' Annie felt guilty now and even more uncomfort-able. Tom obviously thought she was being selfish and vain, keeping a ten-dollar gold piece all for herself when the family was in need. He had gone very silent now and was watching her closely.

'Father is keeping it safe for me. I'll ask him about it and perhaps if he thinks it's a good idea . . . ' she said lamely. But Tom quickly interjected.

'No, Annie, no, don't say anything to Father. He wouldn't understand this. He doesn't know much about money. Don't mention it to him. We'll talk about it again.'

With that Tom changed the subject entirely and diverted her with stories about his job at the hotel and all the fine people who came to stay there. Annie soon forgot their conversation and it was not until some weeks later that she would have reason to recall it.

By the time they got back to the beach, the family was about ready to leave. They'd had a marvellous time and Father had a bucket of clams. 'We'll bake them in the stove when we get home,' he promised.

It was a goodly walk to the giant fairgrounds but well worth the journey.

'Roll up, roll up, a nickel a go!' The enormous roller-coaster circling around and around and higher and higher was a thrilling spectacle and the boys clamoured to go on it but Father said he wouldn't risk his children's lives on such a dangerous machine, and they were soon pacified with a promise of a treat from one of the numerous booths. Sweet potatoes, hot dogs, salt-water taffy, fruit, peanuts, jelly apples or ice cream – they could take their pick.

Spellbound, they watched a fire-eating lady, a black-and-white minstrel show and bare-knuckled boxers, all within the space of half-an-hour. There was so much to see and do that they could have been there for a month. By the time they had been on the swingboats and car-ousels and tried their hand at the shooting galleries, it was nearly time to head back for the excursion boat.

What a day they'd had. The fresh sea air had blown all their heat fatigue and worries away. They felt as if they'd been away on a holiday. And in a sense, they had. By the time they reached Monroe Street, it was nearly midnight. Philip was fast asleep on Father's shoulders, worn out with the fun and excitement of the day. Annie fell asleep with a kaleidoscope of images whirling around her head and dreamt she was a fire-eater performing at the Opera House in Cork.

Yes, the family excursion to Coney Island had been a great success.

8

A Difficult Dilemma

The rest of the summer sped by in a haze of heat, and Annie found that her fellow workers in the laundry had not been exaggerating about the unbearable conditions at work during those months. She had to bring a spare petticoat and dress to change into before she returned home in the evenings as her work clothes were wet through with steam and sweat after the day's work.

Annie's only escape during these months was a lofty perch on the fire escape of 32 Monroe Street, where she had taken to sitting for a while late at night with Anthony and Philip, who now slept out there most nights. She had been amazed at first at the sight of tenants carrying their bedding out on the roofs and fire escapes to spend the nights, but as the temperatures grew more oppressive and the tenement rooms like ovens, she longed to do so herself. But Father drew the line at letting his one and only daughter sleep out on the roof. It wouldn't be seemly for a well-brought-up Cork girl to do such a thing, he insisted.

Another very amusing diversion was visiting the public baths with Sophia on a day allotted to women. It was the greatest fun and so refreshing after the scorching furnace of the city. It was after such a swim as they strolled home one evening that Sophia broke the news. 'I didn't want to tell you until I was sure, Annie, but now Papa says I may and I know you'll be happy for me . . .' she looked at her friend, whose eyes were wide with expectation.

'It's the nursing,' broke in Annie excitedly. 'I know it is. You'll be leaving.'

'How did you know?' Sophia's dark eyes widened in amazement. 'Yes, it is. You know I was wrong about Papa. He does want me to have the same chances as the others and when Josef passed his examinations last month he told me I could apply for training in a hospital. So I applied to Bellevue and they'll take me in October because I'll be seventeen by then.'

'Oh Sophia, I'm so pleased but – ' Annie stopped and her face changed comically to a mock tragic expression ' – how am I going to live without you? It will be so lonesome at the laundry.'

Her friend laughed. 'Don't worry, you'll be fine. Anyway the hospital is here in New York and I'll be allowed home every so often. But Annie, now it's your turn. You've got to get yourself out of the laundry and get a better job. Remember how many times you became ill last winter. Mama says that once you get a bad chest, you'll never get rid of it and you could even get consumption. And the laundry will never change. Mr Dunbar will never improve things.'

'I know that, Sophia, that's what Mother says too but it's not so easy,' replied Annie. 'I don't want to stay home and make money as a seamstress. It wouldn't pay well enough and besides I would be locked up at home and never see the outside world. From what I hear a factory job would be every bit as bad as the laundry.

'I might go into service. Mother is trying to get me a position through her friend, Sister Bonaventure. It's not my dearest wish but I think I might be able to have a better life if I got settled with a family. Then I could take some night classes. Even the boys are doing classes a couple of nights a week so they can learn a trade. Philip's learning stitching so he can help Mother with her work at home and Anthony's learning shoemaking. I really want to learn more, Sophia. In Ireland I was learning French and music and all sorts. '

Sophia looked sympathetic. Then she smiled wickedly. 'And poetry. What about poetry, Annie? Oh no, I forgot, you learn that when you come to America, eh? 'she teased.

Annie chased her friend all the way down the street and around the corner. Suddenly, just as she drew level with her, they almost collided with a figure running towards them. As they recovered themselves, Annie saw that it was Tom, looking terrified and seemingly running away from a burly man who had just emerged from a doorway shouting, 'Come back you scoundrel. You lousy cheat, you try to honeyfuggle me. You'll not get away with this. I'll fix your flint, so I will!'

Tom, who must have seen the girls, didn't even stop to speak to his sister, just scarpered off around the corner and was gone.

'It was Tom! Did you see him, Sophia?' Annie looked shocked. 'What was he doing?' A number of rather well-dressed men had now gathered at the same door which, looking up, the girls perceived to be a gentleman's club of some kind. 'Faro Bank' was written in black lettering over the door.

Seeing the girls stop and look so taken aback, one of the men approached and asked if they were all right. Sophia, not wishing to get involved, pulled at Annie's sleeve. 'Come, Annie. Let us get along home.'

But Annie, intensely curious at this stage, boldly replied, 'Thank you, Sir. We are fine. But what happened? Was that a thief running away?'

'You could say that, young lady. A lying, cheating thief. Tonight, he was caught red-handed. We've been after him for some time. It's the last time he'll be let into any of our clubs I can tell you. He'll be blacklisted.' The gentleman, lifting his hat, re-entered the club.

'Annie, please, please,' Sophia was nearly in tears by now. 'Don't you see, it's a gambling club. Come, let us get home.' She pulled her friend away from the scene.

Annie had turned deathly pale. 'I can't believe it, Sophia. What could Tom be thinking of? What shall I do?'

The two girls hurried away, Annie now clutching Sophia's arm for support. 'What will Father say? He will kill Tom.' Annie shivered at the thought.

'Look, Annie, the best thing is not to say anything until you know some more. Perhaps it's all a mistake. Don't tell your father yet. If Tom is in as much trouble as that, he'll soon be up before the courts and then your father will know all about it.'

Annie listened to her friend, almost too upset to take in what she was saying. They fell silent for the rest of the walk home.

That night Annie slept hardly a wink. The scene kept playing over and over again in her mind. Tom running like mad, the look of horror on his face, the man running out the door of the club, purple-faced with anger, the contempt on the face of the man she spoke to about Tom.

She had to accept that Tom was certainly in some sort of trouble. He had come running out of a gambling club – that's what Sophia said it was. Faro was a card game men played for money, she knew that. So Tom was gambling then? She wished she could tell someone about it. No, Sophia was right, she shouldn't tell her father right now. She would confront Tom. Yes, that's what she would do. After work some night this week, she would stop at the hotel he worked at downtown and ask to see him. If he wasn't there, she would leave a message with the Head Porter. She simply had to speak to him. There might have been some mistake. But the more she thought about it, the more she knew it was not a mistake. Suddenly she remembered their great day at Coney Island and how Tom had tried to persuade her to give him her special ten-dollar gold piece she'd got when she came to America. 'Your eagle, Annie. Have you still got your golden eagle?' And how he'd backed off when she'd said that Father was minding it. Yes, Tom was in trouble all right.

It was another two weeks before Annie got the opportunity to follow up the events of that evening. A more pressing matter had taken her attention in the intervening days. Mother had been taken ill and was rushed into hospital late one night.

Annie discovered only then that her mother had been expecting a baby which would have been due in four months' time. Sadly, she had begun haemorrhaging and within hours Father had returned from the City Hospital with the news that Mother had lost the baby. It was no surprise to Annie that Mother was ill enough to be kept a few days in hospital. She had thought her mother had not looked at all well for some time, but she was quite shocked to learn that another child was on the way and she had not even known about it.

Annie wished again that it was not necessary for Mother to work so hard. She knew her parents were struggling to make a better life for the family and that every dollar counted. It was an anxious time and Father appeared quite worried and preoccupied about it. Annie knew for sure now that she just couldn't tell him the news about Tom. No, she would have to try and deal with it herself. But what if Tom were arrested or put in prison? How would the family manage without the financial support he had been giving?

When Mother returned home a few days later she looked very pale and tired but her spirits were good and the family's worries were eased a little when she announced that she would not be taking in any further piecework for a little while. The doctor had advised that she was ruining her health.

'We'll manage right fine now, Mary, don't you even think of it,' Father reassured her. 'Anyway, I'm hoping for promotion any day now.'

During all this time, Tom had not been home and did not even know his mother had been taken ill, so Annie thought it was high time she spoke to him. The following evening after work she went straight to the Excelsior Hotel off Fifth Avenue where Tom worked. It was a long way from the laundry and in order not to waste too much time she took a streetcar. Annie disliked the streetcars. They were nearly always full to overflowing and she felt sorry for the poor unfortunate horses who had to carry such a heavy load. A month previously she had seen with her own eyes a horse collapse and almost overturn an overcrowded car on Broadway.

Besides, some of the passengers were often rowdy or even drunk and it was well known that pickpockets got their richest pickings on the streetcars. Tonight, she reached her destination quickly and safely and stepped down from the car not far from the hotel.

Annie had only been there once but she remembered that she should approach the desk and ask for the porter's office. Entering the lobby, however, she immediately saw Tom, who looked very professional and confident in his bell-hop uniform – dark red with black edging on trousers and jacket and black cap – and for a moment she was stricken with a terrible doubt. Perhaps she'd been mistaken, perhaps it hadn't been Tom at all that evening. But no, she knew she was right. She had not made a mistake.

'Annie, what brings you here at all?' Tom had caught sight of her and came over immediately. 'Is everything all right?'

'Can we talk, Tom,' Annie asked. 'Away from here,' she added, looking around her at the busy hotel lobby. She would have loved the hustle and bustle on any other occasion.

'Well, I'm working, but we can have a few minutes. Come in here then.' He steered her into a small room near the porter's desk. It was full of luggage. He had a quick word with the uniformed man at the desk and followed her in, shutting the door behind him. Annie wasted no time. She had decided to be very blunt.

'Look, Tom, I saw you that night running away from the club. What was happening? Did you not see me?'

Tom's face registered shock for a split second and then he smiled one of his charming smiles and said simply, 'I don't know what you're talking about, Sis. What club?'

Annie felt helpless. It was obvious that Tom was not going to admit a thing. She described to him what she had seen and he completely denied having been anywhere near such a place. She was very upset at the turn things had taken, but in the face of such total denial all she could do was change the subject and tell him the news about Mother's illness.

He was clearly upset. 'I should have been home last week, Annie, but I didn't have enough money put by to give them and I felt so badly . . . ' he tailed off weakly, the first time Annie had ever seen Tom stuck for words. She left soon afterwards with Tom's blessing for Mother and his promise that he would return home on his next day off. Nothing further was said.

'It was just as though I had imagined it all,' she confided in Sophia next day at work. 'I don't know what to do now. I'm so angry with him, Sophia, yet he's my brother. I love him and I know he has great good in him. I fear, though, he's changed and it's too late to do anything. I don't want to worry Father right now. He has enough to worry about.'

It was now September, Annie's favourite month by far. It was still quite hot in New York but after the sizzling temperatures of July and August, it seemed quite bearable. Mother was back on her feet again and, now that she didn't have to slave at the needlework, was a changed woman. She looked so much better and was in higher spirits than Annie had ever seen her. She talked about starting up work again soon but Annie hoped she wouldn't have to. They all waited eagerly for Father to get the long-awaited promotion at the factory. She had not seen Tom since the night at the hotel but he had been home as he promised, although always while Annie was at work. Obviously, he was still able to make his contribution to the household – if he hadn't, she would surely have heard about it. She hoped he had come by it honestly but she was full of doubts.

At the laundry, five women had been sacked for protesting about work conditions. Nobody replaced them. Annie worried about keeping her job as everybody seemed to be under suspicion since that incident. Alice Rodgers spent every dinner hour trying to pacify and reassure the workers that everything would be all right.

Sophia would be leaving shortly and Annie dreaded the thought of life at the laundry without her. Josef too would shortly depart to take up his studies at the Rabbinate. Annie looked up to him more than ever and envied Sophia her clever and successful big brother. She could never imagine Josef doing what Tom had done.

She worried constantly about Tom but deep down she felt powerless to find a solution. She told no one about it and she and Sophia no longer spoke about it. Sophia was very excited about her own plans and couldn't think or talk about anything else.

Annie was greatly cheered around this time to receive letters from both Ellie King in Nebraska and her old friend Julia Donohue in Cork. Ellie broke the exciting news that she had met a young man and would marry him next Spring. He was Irish also.

> I'm really happy, [wrote Ellie]. We have plans to farm and bring up our family out here. Life here, I'm sure, is dull compared to New York but I love the wide open spaces. It's hard in winter as the climate is cruel but people are good and I have made some staunch and loyal friends. I hope some day you'll come visit and see for yourself.

Julia, on the other hand, was not in such a happy frame of mind.

> Cork hasn't changed one bit since you left nearly a year ago. How I miss you, Annie. And how I envy your new life in America. It sounds so exciting. I know your job is hard but it must be fine to be independent. I do not know what I will do with my life. You're lucky to have finished with school and lessons. I'm looking forward to finishing at the Convent next June but I don't know what I might do as there are not many jobs for girls in Cork. Sister Mary Catherine says I would make a good nun. I won't do it, I told Mother, even though she prays for it every day. I'd like to train to be a singer but Father

> *couldn't afford that. Please write soon. I like to hear*
> *about your life.*

Reading this brought it home to Annie how very much her life had changed in the past year, how much she had seen and how much more she knew about life than she would if she had stayed in Cork. And although she often became homesick for Ireland and missed her aunt and uncle and Julia, it occurred to her for the first time that, given the chance right now, she would not turn back the clock.

9
—

A Friend in Need

'Ladies first.' Annie almost collided with the man who held the school door open for her. Already twenty minutes late collecting Philip from night school, she barely glanced at him as she muttered 'thank-you' but something in his tone of voice or what he said caused her to look up just as she passed him. She found herself looking straight into the smiling face of Mike Tierney, the young man who had been so kind to her on her voyage from Ireland so many months ago.

'Well if it isn't Miss Annie Moore – the famous Golden-Dollar Girl herself,' laughed Mike, taking her hand and shaking it as if it were the village pump.

'Mike Tierney!' Annie exclaimed. 'I'm so happy to see you, Mike.' And she was indeed delighted. She had liked Mike from the first and remembered that it was entirely due to him that she had been fêted as the first immigrant to arrive off the ferry-boat at Ellis Island on New Year's Day.

That was it, the way he had said 'Ladies first' had jogged her memory and brought back how he had first uttered those very words to the big German who had tried to push her aside, alighting from the ferry at Ellis Island on that momentous occasion.

'But tell me, what are you doing here? The classes are finished for the evening now.'

'I've come for Philip,' replied Annie.

At this point Philip appeared from the corner of the lobby where he had been anxiously awaiting his sister. He looked a little sheepish until understanding dawned on Mike's face.

'Of course – the little brothers who were with you. I didn't know you, Philip, you've grown so much. Sure I'm teaching him, aren't I?' he turned to Annie.

'Are you?' Annie was astonished. Philip had been coming to the night classes for a few weeks already and had never mentioned his teacher. But he hadn't recognised Mike either, it turned out.

'But I thought you were a tailor,' Annie said.

'Indeed and I am,' replied Mike, as they strolled down the street together. 'But I teach too – night classes in stitching and upholstery. But tell me, what are you doing yourself? How are you getting along?'

In no time at all Annie had told Mike all that had happened to her since she had arrived in America. Somehow she instinctively trusted him. It was like meeting an old friend from home but one who knew all about life over here too. And that was something Annie lacked in her new life. By the time they reached the end of the street, Annie knew that Mike lived and worked in the garment district down on Seventh Avenue and 34th Street, near some of the fashionable department stores and that he worked as a junior cutter for quite a big fashion house there.

'It's hard work but I hope to continue at it and open my own business one day,' Mike confided.

Before they parted she made him promise to call to Monroe Street the very next Sunday to meet the family.

She returned home feeling pleased as punch and hoped that Mike had noticed how much she'd grown up since he'd last seen her. She always wore her hair up now – sure wasn't she nearly sixteen.

It was now nearing the end of September and the whole of New York could talk of nothing else but the marvellous celebrations set to take place in October for the 400th anniversary of the discovery of America by Christopher Columbus. There would be parades and fireworks and marches and speeches and fairs throughout the country for one full week. The Wednesday of that week was declared a legal holiday as it fell on 12 October, which was the true anniversary of the day in 1492 when the great Italian navigator had discovered America. That was going to be the best day of all, with a mighty military parade during the day and the unveiling of the Columbus Monument in Central Park, followed by a night-time pageant in the city streets, which, according to all the newspapers, would be more splendid than anything New York had ever seen before.

Father read all the latest details to them every night from the newspaper. 'They've forgotten that there's a presidential election only a few weeks after it,' grumbled Father, shaking his head. 'They'll all be too tuckered out to vote.' In truth, Father was far more interested in the political situation and supported the Democrats' candidate, Grover Cleveland, over President Benjamin Harrison who was the Republicans' candidate. Therefore, he was very pleased indeed that when Mike Tierney paid his first visit to the family he turned out not only to be interested in politics but active into the bargain.

Mike spent a lot of his spare time working down at Tammany Hall helping the Democratic Party. He had even met the famous Boss Croker. Father was mightily impressed. He chuckled with delight when Mike told him of the infamous 'tiger's' doings. Annie was fascinated. All she knew of politics was the talk she heard down at the laundry about tariffs and low wages and cheap labour and how the government did nothing but break its promises. She never thought it could be fun. But this sounded mighty exciting.

'It's sure we'll get Cleveland in,' Mike told her father confidently. 'Four years of the Republicans has not paid off. Harrison's licked for certain.'

Annie was sorry Tom wasn't there that day as she was sure he'd like Mike and see what a fine fellow he was. Then she was struck by a brilliant idea. She would confide in Mike about Tom – he'd be the very person to know what to do. Having met her family, he'd know that they were honest, good people and that deep down Tom wasn't a cheat.

So it was that the next evening the boys were at night-class, Annie contrived to call by to accompany them home but with the intention of speaking privately to Mike. It wouldn't do to have her young brothers know anything of this.

Just about to lock up his classroom, Mike looked

surprised to see her but smiled his welcome. Annie wasted no time. She was conscious of Mike being a teacher and she didn't know him well enough to presume she could trifle with his time so she came to the point right away.

'Mike, I have a problem. I couldn't speak to you about it last Sunday in front of my parents. They don't know anything about it.' She paused, embarrassed. Mike listened attentively.

'It's my brother Tom. He's in trouble.' She spilled out the whole story, right down to her recent effort to talk to Tom. Mike listened with a grave expression, and when she finished there was a brief silence.

'He could end up in serious trouble if he's gambling and cheating, Annie,' Mike said seriously. 'It sounds as if he has lost a lot of money or that he's in trouble with someone else. He may owe a large sum. It doesn't sound as if he would cheat for the hell of it.'

'No, Mike, I'm sure of it. Tom is honest at heart and wouldn't wish anyone ill. But is there any way you can help me at all? I truly don't know where to turn, I'm that worried about him.'

'I'll have to think about it, Annie. I would have to find out what he's up to exactly before I could be of any help.'

Annie brightened. 'Perhaps if I could let you know when he will next visit home and you could come along and . . . '

'No, Annie, that wouldn't do at all. He would not likely confide in me at all if he meets me with the family. No, it's best if I approach this in another way. I know the Excelsior Hotel. I can find out more if I act quietly and alone. Do you trust me to do that?'

Looking up at him, Annie knew she'd trust him with her life. There was something so strong and confident about him. Her heart lifted for the first time in weeks, and she felt as if a heavy burden had just been lifted off her shoulders.

'I trust you, Mike,' she replied simply.

'Good,' said Mike, smiling again. 'Come by for the boys again next week and perhaps I'll be able to tell you something. And don't fret any more. Get on home now, and let me finish off here. I haven't time to be wasting with golden-dollar wenches.'

Annie laughed, made a saucy face at him and skipped off home with the boys, feeling happy and carefree. What a friend Mike was turning out to be.

In the first week of October the sense of excitement about the Columbus Day celebrations grew to fever pitch. Mother, for once not overworked and exhausted, was helping out on a committee formed to decorate the neighbourhood streets and already there was enough brightly coloured bunting adorning the gas lamps on Monroe Street to hang right across America. Down at the laundry, the women temporarily forgot their grievances and at dinner hour the talk was only about the festivities ahead. The greatest worry was that even on the legal holiday Mr Dunbar might insist they come to work. Annie prayed she'd be free to enjoy the fun on that day.

She hoped Mother would have her dress ready. Mother had been making Annie a new winter dress from some leftover material she'd put aside before she fell ill. Annie longed for a bell skirt topped by a tucked shirtwaist which was all the fashion nowadays and worn by those smart young women she often saw in the more fashionable areas of town. She knew such an outfit would make her look nearly eighteen. She wished she could afford to have her likeness taken in her new dress by one of the latest Kodak cameras to send home to Ireland. But she'd heard it cost too much so she guessed she'd have to make do with a daguerrotype portrait for the time being.

The days passed and Annie heard nothing from Mike. He wasn't at the night school on the one evening she managed to call by. Had he been able to talk to Tom, she wondered. Even more important, had Tom talked to Mike? Perhaps this was the wrong way to go about things. Mike was a complete stranger to Tom, after all, and he might resent such an approach. He might even insult Mike and start a fight with him. She agonised over it endlessly and wished she had never mentioned the whole sorry business to Mike at all.

She was finally put out of her agony when she came out of the laundry one evening after work and found none other than Mike waiting for her on the sidewalk.

'Mike!' She started anxiously towards him.

'What has you looking so worried, lass?' asked Mike, leaning casually against the railings with his arms crossed, smiling at her as if he had all the time in the world. Annie saw he had a twinkle in his eye and felt a surge of hope.

'Have you . . . did you speak to Tom, then?' she asked.

'Speak to Tom, is it? Why would I speak to him? Oh yes, you told me about some problem he had, didn't you? Now let me see, did I speak to him?'

Annie could see he was teasing her and wanted to shake him. 'Mike, please tell me, please. What happened?'

Mike burst out laughing. 'The look on your face! Sorry, Annie, I just couldn't resist it. Yes is the answer to your question. I spoke to him all right, but a lot happened before I got to do that, I can tell you.'

As they strolled along Annie heard the whole story. She heard how Mike had gone to the hotel and identified Tom – he hadn't spoken to him then, just found out what he looked like – and how a few nights later he spotted Tom leaving the hotel one night and followed him.

'I felt badly, Annie, following him like that, but it was the only way to try and find out more,' said Mike.

Apparently, Tom had gone into a rather seedy-looking saloon somewhere in the back streets behind the hotel and reappeared about twenty minutes later with two men. They had all burst through the door, the other men propelling a terrified-looking Tom in front of them.

'I was watching from a doorway and they didn't see me at all. They started to beat him up in the alleyway at the side of the club.'

'Oh no, poor Tom,' interjected Annie, appalled.

'They had already beaten him some, in fact,' explained Mike. 'because he was bleeding badly, but they were obviously going to finish the job outside. One of them shouted at him to give them the money or something like that. Then they threw him on the ground and . . . '

Seeing Annie looking really distressed at this point, Mike abandoned any further gory details. 'He's fine now, Annie, don't fret,' he interjected quickly. 'As soon as I saw what was happening I ran over, shouting at the top of my voice for help and I think they got such a fright they took off straight away.'

Annie, looking at Mike, thought how strong-looking he was – no wonder the villains had scarpered.

'He was in a mess all right, poor lad – they were right ruffians, but I got him to the hospital in a hackney cab and they looked after him right away. He had to stay a day or two mind, he got a bad gash on his eye. He didn't know who I was but he was so confused that night that I couldn't talk with him at all.'

Annie looked crestfallen until Mike reassured her that he went to visit Tom the next day, telling him he was a friend of Annie's.

'I got talking to him then and probably because he knew I'd got him out of a bad scrape or because he was so weak, he broke down and told me everything. You were right, Annie, he's been gambling and got out of his depth. Then when the losses mounted up he started cheating. Eventually, he had to borrow money from a lender and of course he couldn't pay it back. He's got thrown out of several clubs on account of the cheating and now the lender is after him – that's who was set on beating him up.'

Annie wrung her hands. 'Oh, what am I going to do, Mike? Will I have to tell my parents about it after all?'

'Hold on, hold on, Annie, I've not finished. It's all been looked after. It's solved now,' Mike soothed her.

Mike related then how he had proposed a plan to Tom to help him out of this difficult situation. Mike, it appeared, had friends in Tammany Hall who could give Tom a loan to pay off his debt. In return, Tom would have to give over a lot of his spare time to helping out with the presidential campaign over the coming weeks.

'Of course he first had to promise me never to get into that kind of mess again,' Mike said. 'But you know, Annie, he's a grand fellow really, is Tom. I don't think he meant to get in so deep in the first place. We've talked a lot over the past few days and got to know each other. I think it would be wise if you didn't mention anything about this business to him. He's bitterly ashamed, deep down. I think he'll be a great help to us. He's as smart as two pins, just like his sister,' he added, smiling at her.

'So it's all solved then?' Annie looked incredulous. 'Mike, you're a marvel.' She stopped abruptly and looked up at him, her admiration plain. Here was this man she hardly knew, who had smoothed the way for her from the first minute she met him on the voyage from Ireland. She hadn't laid eyes on him for months but he had now reappeared and in one fell swoop, simply because she had asked him, had solved the most vexing problem she had ever had to deal with. And not only that, it seemed he and Tom had even become friends.Without stopping to think, she flung her arms around his neck and gave him a warm hug. She just couldn't help it. 'Thank you, thank you, thank you,' she cried.

Mike swung her around. 'Hey what's this, young Annie,' he laughed, putting her down and holding her at arm's length. 'Take it easy or people will think you're my sweetheart.'

At this Annie blushed to the roots of her hair and blurted out, 'And have you got one then?'

'Sure, I've got about twenty of 'em,' laughed Mike, 'but

I'll put you top of the list if you like.'

Still laughing, they parted, he having promised to come and visit again shortly at Monroe Street. Relieved and happy as Annie was about Tom being rescued, all she could think about was Mike. How handsome he was, she thought. Her embarrassment at having hugged him was forgotten as she pondered whether he had been pleased or not. She couldn't decide. Heavens, Auntie Norah would have been shocked had she seen her. 'Forward,' she would have called her. But Mike deserved a hug for all he'd done for her, she thought, smiling to herself. Maybe he'd accompany them to the pageant next week. She hoped to goodness Mother would have her dress ready by then.

'Watch out,' called a passer-by sharply as Annie, stepping dreamily out off the sidewalk, nearly collided with a street peddler on the corner of Hester Street.

10

ELECTION FEVER

Dear Uncle Charlie and Auntie Norah

It's been the best week I've had in America! As you know – I'm sure Father has already written and told you – America is celebrating its 400th Anniversary and the most special day of all was Wednesday as that was the very day Christopher Columbus discovered the New World in 1492. Everyone here has been talking about it for months and preparing and all. It all began for us on Monday when Anthony took part in the big schools parade, and he the only boy in his class to march. We were proud fit to bursting. Sad it was that I was at work and Father too, and couldn't see it all but Mother and Philip went and cheered.

Most workers were given Wednesday off and although we had to go to work as usual in the morning we had high hopes to be left off early. And we were. 'Twas a miracle that Mr Dunbar agreed though some say it was only for he might attract attention from the wrong quarters if he kept us *working. The only thing he's afraid of, they say, is the inspectors – that they might see how bad he treats us. Thank goodness we were let go at eleven o'clock.*

I ran all the way to the corner of Madison Square Gardens to meet the family so as to watch the grand military parade. I nearly missed them as the crowds were so great and everyone pushing to get the best place. I thought I'd die. But I found them at last. Tom was there and all so it was the whole family together for the first time since the day at Coney Island in the summer.

The best sight of all was the gigantic model of Columbus's ship – it took a whole team of horses to pull it – followed by a statue of Columbus himself holding a cross. Later on we went to see the pageant and I am glad we did as that was the best part of the whole day.

You've heard tell I think of our friend Mike Tierney who helped me on the voyage over. He's the nicest man you could meet and so fine-looking. But you don't be worrying Auntie Norah, he's Tom's friend too and I'm really glad of it for he's got Tom to help him in the election which is taking place here next month for a new president. Leastways Mike is sure there's to be a new president because he works for the Democrats but there are those as would say that the Republican president we have will do nicely again.

In any case Mike has friends in the New York Herald *and he invited us to come along to their*

office on Broadway where we could watch all the
goings-on from the fourth floor. We felt like the
gentry and Mike's friends made us right welcome.
Oh I can't explain what it was like to be up there
above the crowds and to be able to see it all! There
were flame-throwers and clowns and all manner of
novelties and amusing people marching and dancing
in the street below. It went on for hours and we all
loved the fireworks – there were Roman candles,
rockets and bombs – which would shoot up into the
dark and fall like a shower of beautiful colours
lighting up the place for miles around.

I wore my new dress that Mother made me and
I felt like a true lady. I plan to send you my likeness
taken in my finery for Christmas so you can see how
I've grown up since you last saw me.

Hoping this finds you as it leaves me
Your loving niece Annie

After the celebrations, Annie's life resumed its normal
routine, only now without the enjoyment of Sophia's
company and all it entailed – visits to the Rostov's house
and to Papa Rostov's junk shop where she had so enjoyed
browsing among the books with Josef and drinking tea.
Sophia had started her studies at the hospital and Josef
had departed for the Rabbinate. Suddenly life seemed
empty and grey, and the prospect of facing into another
winter working at the laundry was daunting. Mike Tierney
often came to visit on Sundays and Annie looked forward
immensely to his company, but much as she liked to think
she was special to him, she couldn't help but notice that

he seemed to enjoy her father's and Tom's company just as much as hers. If only she knew more about the dratted politics!

But try as she might she could not interest herself in the approaching election with anything like Tom's new-found fervour. He now spent almost all of his spare time working down at Tammany Hall with Mike and they talked endlessly of 'the campaign'. She would be glad when it was all over. After yet another feverish discussion around the Moore's kitchen table one evening just days before the presidential election was to take place, Annie was surprised when Mike asked her if she could spare any time to help him.

'I could really be doing with your help, Annie, if you had a little time to spare after work,' Mike said in a serious tone – not his usual bantering manner – and Annie sat up attentively on the settle. 'I need people to distribute flimsies over the next couple of days. If you could help at all I'd be obliged.'

Mike smiled at her puzzled expression. 'Flimsies are leaflets telling all about our candidates and saying why people should vote for them. You'd just have to hand them to the passers-by.'

Annie agreed and so it was that she found herself reporting to Tammany Hall on Frankfort Street early on the Sunday morning before the election. She was amazed to find the place full of noise and activity. People seemed to be rushing in every direction and there was Mike like a general, marshalling his troops in the big room upstairs. He hailed her briefly and motioned to her to join the crowd of young men and women helpers he was addressing.

Annie now saw a new side to Mike as he spoke to them – he was not stern yet he exuded a certain amount of authority.

'I want you to go out in pairs and cover all the streets in this area,' he was saying. 'Deliver to all the houses and to all the people you meet. Now let me state clearly that only the young men are to enter the saloons to distribute the flimsies. I want no young women to be seen next or near a saloon in any circumstances. Do not respond if anyone tries to pick a fight with you or argue with you. Your job is to deliver this information. Good then, I'll see you all back here in a couple of hours and there will be something to eat and then we can get to work again in the afternoon.'

Annie was paired off with a girl about her own age called Molly O'Byrne. Molly's parents, it turned out, were from County Limerick and had come to America before Molly was born. She was a bright, lively sort of girl and Annie immediately felt at home with her. By the time the morning's work was over Annie had begun to enjoy herself greatly and had become as adept as Molly at pushing leaflets into even the most unwilling hands, calling out 'Vote for Cleveland – The Best Man For The Job – Grover Cleveland For President!' Returning at lunchtime to Tammany Hall, she had rid herself of her entire bundle, earning an admiring look from Mike.

'We'll make a Democrat of you yet, Annie,' he teased.

By the end of the day she felt she was an old hand, and she and Molly returned to Tammany Hall which was now abuzz with hectic preparations for the last giant rally to be held that evening. All the political bigwigs had arrived and Annie had the good luck to have the famous Boss Croker pointed out to her on the stairway – the infamous 'tiger' her father talked of. How thrilled he'll be that I saw him, she thought.

Tom was there in the thick of things as Mike's right-hand man, and Annie was proud of her brother. He seemed to have changed and matured so much recently. 'Howdee Sis' was all he had time for as he rushed hither and thither. The rally was to start at eight o'clock and Annie and Molly found themselves swept up in the activity of preparing the magnificent great hall for the event.

By eight o'clock the level of excitement was feverish, and at Mr Cleveland's arrival, the hall exploded into wild cheering and applause as he took the podium for his final pre-election address. At the edge of the crowd which spilled out onto the street neither Annie nor Molly could hear much of what he said but were carried along by the general sense of elation.

'And they say his wife is the most beautiful lady in all America,' Molly told Annie, after they'd heard Mr Cleveland open with sympathetic words for his rival, President Harrison, whose wife had finally succumbed to her illness and died a few days previously.

Privately Annie thought if women had the vote and she was of age she'd certainly vote for Mr Harrison, if only to make up for the poor man's terrible trouble. But looking around at this crowd she knew it would be seen as heresy to say as much.

'How did you come to be interesting yourself in this kind of thing, Molly?' asked Annie as the two girls walked some of the way home together later in the evening.

''Tis my father, he's been a supporter for years,' explained Molly. 'And my brothers are in it too. So if you have a word to say in our house it has to be about politics – especially when there's an election coming up,' she added.

It emerged that Molly was seventeen and had just finished school in a convent in Brooklyn. She was about to start training to be a schoolteacher.

'You're fortunate,' said Annie enviously. 'My parents only came over a few years ago. I only came myself last January and we're still making our way so we must all work.' She told Molly about her job in the laundry and how she hoped to get out of it this year and into domestic service. 'I can't say as how I would wish to be anyone's servant,' she explained, 'but I'm not trained for anything and leastways I'd see my way to going to night classes in my time off. There's not a lot I can do about the learning while I work in that laundry.'

She began to confide in Molly about the long hours and difficult conditions. Molly looked shocked as she listened, and Annie knew instinctively that Molly came from a more comfortable background than her own. But she was sympathetic and direct and Annie liked her for that. It no longer hurt Annie's pride to admit that she was a working girl – she was quite proud of it really – but she felt keenly that she had been deprived in some way and she now appreciated how well she'd been educated before she left Cork. An American girl like Molly would abhor the idea of going into service, she knew, but then as Father often said 'beggars can't be choosers', and she was quite resigned to her fate for the moment.

Parting at the station where Molly would catch her train home to Brooklyn, they arranged to meet on election night a few days later.

'It will be even more fun than this evening, Annie – you'll see,' promised Molly, and she was proved right.

Tom accompanied Annie and Molly to Madison Square Gardens on election night, where the Democrat supporters would wait long into the night for the results.

'Wait until you see. They will flash the results from the tower and you will be able to see the illuminations in Brooklyn,' explained Tom.

'If that's so, I should have stayed home this evening,' quipped Molly, who had no inhibitions about cheeking Annie's big brother.

'Well, Miss O'Byrne, you might find yourself doing just that if you don't behave now,' retorted Tom, who found Molly's bright personality much to his liking.

Very different looking from Annie, Molly was petite with jet-black straight hair scraped back into a topknot and merry brown eyes. Tonight she wore a pert little hat cocked at an angle and looked a picture.

There were thousands of people already there when they arrived, and there was a great mood of expectation as results began to come in. They appeared to be over-whelmingly favourable for the Democrats and were greeted with much cheering and joviality. Annie was fascinated to see how the latest news was relayed to the crowds by a giant flashlight from the top of the tower just as Tom had described. As the evening progressed it appeared that their candidate might even have a landslide victory, so even though they wouldn't know the final result until morning, the three young people went home happy.

Being involved in the election campaign had been so much more fun than Annie had thought possible, as well as which she had made a new friend.

11

ANOTHER NEW YORK WINTER

'Sophia, at last. I'm so happy to see you.' Coming out of the laundry one foggy afternoon in November, Annie was thrilled to see her friend eagerly scanning the women's faces to pick her out.

'It's my first Saturday off and I may stay home until tomorrow morning,' Sophia explained, linking her arm into Annie's. 'I've so much to tell you. Let's walk to Papa's shop and have a cup of tea.'

'I love the hospital, Annie, but it's such hard work – almost worse than the laundry,' confided Sophia once they were settled in Papa Rostov's cosy little office at the back of the shop. 'We must learn so much and at the same time we have to assist at operations and help bleed the patients. Then when there are emergencies during the night they will always call one or two of us out of bed to help, even though we are not supposed to be on night duty. But we can take turns. I have seen some frightening cases already.'

Annie was enthralled. It was evident that despite her complaints her friend found her work exciting and satisfying. She ached with envy at the new life Sophia was describing. Maybe some day she too would be able to work at something she loved.

Annie told Sophia about how Mike Tierney had come to Tom's rescue and how it had all ended happily, with Tom and Mike becoming fast friends. She recounted too the fun she'd had working for Mike during the presidential election.

'So you have another admirer, then,' teased Sophia. 'Poor Josef. No sooner has he left than you have given up poetry in favour of politics. Shame on you, Annie.'

Annie blushed. 'How is Josef?' she asked.

'He likes it much better than he thought,' replied Sophia. 'I guess he will be a good rabbi some day after all.'

Papa Rostov, who sorely missed his daughter's cheerful presence at home, made them sit in his warm and cosy office and insisted on serving them tea from the old samovar, which was singing away on the stove as usual.

Settling down with Sophia to chat beside the brightly-glowing stove, Annie felt perfectly contented and for the next couple of hours the friends talked non-stop. Sophia was relieved that she had left the laundry, for from what Annie told her, conditions were getting worse – there had been a near-disaster the week before when one of the big rotary irons overheated and nearly caught fire – and the women were becoming more and more angry and discontented.

'I hate it, Sophia, and I am already seeking a new position, but I must wait until after Christmas when things are a little better at home. Mother has stopped taking in work from Mr Jacobson on account of her health. Mike Tierney has promised to get her a little work if he can so she will at least make some money, and I hope that will come to pass before too long.'

Sophia was pleased that Annie was at least seeking some other work, as she knew there were many things her friend could put her hand to which would be more rewarding. Annie was very bright, anyone could see that, and Sophia felt for her that she could not continue the education she had begun in her home country. However, she was sure that Annie would eventually find her way.

'My goodness, it's seven o'clock, I must get home straight away.' Annie jumped up in dismay. The girls parted with promises to see one another again at Christmas, if not before.

Thanksgiving came and went. Molly had invited Annie to spend it with her family in Brooklyn, but such was the volume of work at the laundry that Annie was not able to accept her invitation. She barely got home in time to catch the tail-end of the special meal Mother had made in honour of the day. Neither was Tom off duty that evening so the Moores' first Thanksgiving as a family passed almost unmarked. Except for one important piece of news. Father's promotion at the factory had come through at last. He had been made supervisor of his floor, which would mean quite a tidy increase. The family talked far into the night about the difference this would make to their lives. Ultimately, it meant only that they could now live a little more comfortably and pay all their bills, but Annie could see that even this was a mighty relief to her parents.

'Can we go live on a farm now?' asked Philip innocently.

'Well, you know, son, we might even do that some day if God is good and all goes well,' said Father, laughing and chucking his youngest under the chin.

That dream was some way away yet but little Philip had managed to hit exactly on what he and Mary hoped would come to pass one day.

Now that winter had set in, Annie had again started to suffer from bronchitis and, although she hadn't missed a day at work so far, she knew that the overheated, damp conditions in which she worked would inevitably lead to more attacks. More and more Annie felt angry at the way they were expected to work at the laundry. She saw how many of the women there suffered under the iron rule of Mr Dunbar, especially women who were pregnant or unwell. She talked to Mike about it one evening he was visiting. For once, to Annie's pleasure, Mike took her absolutely seriously.

'The only way to improve things is to start a trade union,' he began. Mike was himself a member of the Knights of Labor. He explained to Annie that some years ago, a law had been brought into operation which made it illegal for employers to require their workers to work more than sixty hours a week. 'But of course,' he pointed out, 'many employers ignore this, knowing that if they threaten their workers with the loss of their jobs they'll be afraid to complain. That's where a trade union comes in. It means the workers band together to make sure they get treated fairly. An employer will not be afraid to bully one worker but to take them all on – well, he's going to think good and hard.'

Armed with this information, Annie listened more carefully to what the women were saying at work every day. She began to lose patience with Alice Rodgers, who was not really sticking up for the women's rights but helping to keep things from changing. Surely there was a better way to tackle things. So the next time she heard Alice chide a woman who had fumed about the fact that she had been obliged to work late six days in a row for very little extra pay, Annie blurted out, 'It's shocking unfair, so it is!' There was a sudden silence as everyone looked at Annie, the youngest and usually the one who contributed least to this kind of discussion. Gaining in confidence as no-one thought to tell her to be quiet, she continued, 'What we need is a trade union and we have a perfect right to it.'

Alice, shocked, replied, 'Annie, I'm surprised at you. What good would it do? If we asked Mr Dunbar for a trade union we'd be thrown out for sure.'

'Well, he couldn't throw us all out, could he?' retorted Annie. Although everyone laughed, this remark lead to further excited discussion which Alice tried in vain to hush up. Eventually, dinner break came to an end and the inevitable return to work was upon them, but there was a stronger spirit among them and a feeling that something had been started that could not be stopped.

Before she realised it, Annie's first Christmas in America was almost upon her. She delighted in the way the stores were all decorated and the giant outdoor Christmas trees ablaze with the new Edison electric candles. She and Molly had a marvellous time one Satur-day when Annie had finished work, wandering among the throngs of Christmas shoppers. Molly showed her Macy's Christmas window on Sixth Avenue where crowds of people gathered to gasp at the splendid seasonal scenes it depicted.

Annie had never seen anything like it before. It seemed to stretch half-way down the street and was filled with scenes of a snowy wonderland – reindeer drawing sleighs bedecked with holly and red berries, bearing a gloriously rotund Father Christmas. How small and homely it made Cash's in Cork seem.

Another treat was the day she went with Molly – being a native of New York, she knew where everything was – to one of the many daguerrotype salons to have her likeness taken. She had at last managed to save enough overtime money to have it done and was pleased that Molly knew of a salon where they didn't charge a fortune – unlike the famous Mr Brady's salon on Broadway.

When Annie came home after work on Christmas Eve night, it was to a transformation. Mother had decorated the kitchen. She had lowered the wick on the oil lamp on the table and had placed a large Christmas candle in the window which cast a soft glow. She had managed to get some greenery at the market and had decorated the kitchen with it. And in the corner stood a tiny Christmas tree. She had not skimped on the coal and the room was toasty.

Annie had stood stock-still in the doorway. For a moment she thought she was back in Shandon in Auntie Norah's kitchen. 'Mother, it's so pretty,' she began, and suddenly from nowhere tears filled her eyes. For the first time in months she felt acutely homesick. Her mother had somehow recreated the essence of her childhood Christmas and brought home to her for the first time all she had left behind. Seeing her tears, Mother hugged her.

'Dry your eyes now, lass, and I'll show you something grand.' Mother placed a parcel on the table. 'We'll wait for the boys but I can see 'tis from Cork!'

Later, when Annie saw the contents of the parcel and the obvious thought and trouble Auntie Norah and Uncle Charlie had gone to with the choice of their gifts, she shed a few more tears. But the letters from Cork were reassuring, and the arrival of Tom and Mike for Christmas lunch the next day soon dispelled any lingering homesickness She felt lucky to be in America with her family as she recalled the strange and unusual Christmas she'd spent the year before on board the SS *Nevada*.

Funny, she didn't even know Mike then. Now he had become such a good friend to her and the family and had helped them all in so many ways. Looking across the table, she caught his eye and he gave her one of his warmest smiles.

'Glad you came to America then, Annie?' he asked softly.

Annie nodded slowly. She didn't yet know what life held for her here, but right now as she sat in the heart of her family she was indeed glad she had come.

12

A Narrow Escape

It was the beginning of March. Snow lay thick on the ground and Annie, making her way across town to work in the early morning, shivered and pulled her shawl more tightly around her. She had been out of work for the last three days with another attack of bronchitis and felt in no condition to return today, but she feared recriminations from Mrs McCrudden were she to stay at home for another day. Mother, who was expecting another child and feeling well so far, had been keeping an eye on the newspapers' 'Female Help Wanted' column – ever anxious to get her daughter into a better situation – but so far nothing had come of it. She would show Annie the notices every evening when she came in from work.

'Competent girl for general housework, must wear cap and wait on table. Good wages. Call evenings at 1944 Madison Ave., corner 125th St' or 'Girl wanted for upstairs work, wait at table and assist with the washing & ironing. Call before 12.'

Annie had tried for a few of the positions without success and although no one had specifically stated 'No

Irish Need Apply' – words Mike had told her were very often tacked on to the end of these advertisements – she had a sense that it was her nationality that was preventing her from securing a place. But she determined to persevere.

She had thought too of trying to secure a job as a shop assistant but felt that she should really go into service, as board and lodgings would come with the job and with another child expected in the household there would be less and less space at home. It would be some years yet before Anthony and Philip could strike out on their own, but at sixteen she felt it was time for her to do so.

Nothing had improved at the laundry and although the women regularly discussed how to get a trade union started – and Annie was very much part of those discussions since her outburst before Christmas – they had as yet not found a way to do so. Annie knew that it was fear that held them back. Who was she to talk? Here she was shivering in her shoes at the thought of confronting Mrs McCrudden to explain that yes, she had been ill again.

'So, Moore, you have deigned to return and grace us with your presence, have you?' It was worse than she had thought. Mrs McCrudden's piercing tones rang through the ironing hall, causing all heads to turn and look at Annie.

'What have you to say?'

'I am very sorry, Miss, I was ill, truly I was,' replied Annie in what she thought was a humble and respectful tone.

'You don't look ill to me. Perhaps you had better stay late for the next few days and make up all the time you have lost. We don't want to tell Mr Dunbar, do we? It's as well we don't depend on people like you to keep this establishment going.' On and on she went until Annie thought she would die for embarrassment.

As the long afternoon wore on, she found herself becoming more and more angry. How could anyone help it if they were ill? Why was she not believed when she told them she was ill? She had worked hard from the day she had started here and had never told them lies. They behaved as if she was not only a liar but a petty criminal. She couldn't stand it any more. Towards the end of the day, Mrs McCrudden didn't hesitate to remind her that she was to stay on late that night and for the rest of the week. Annie's chest ached and her eyes burned but she bravely approached Mrs McCrudden's high wooden desk and asked if she could please go home as she felt unable to continue. There was a deafening silence.

'I beg your pardon,' thundered Mrs McCrudden.

Annie repeated her request, not faltering one whit.

'Report to Mr Dunbar this instant, do you hear,' Mrs McCrudden roared, her face turning purple with anger. At this, Alice approached the desk with the intention of intervening on Annie's behalf, but it was too late. As if to emphasise her words Mrs McCrudden descended from her podium and, pushing Alice aside, prodded Annie with her hand and pushed her towards the staircase.

Annie, knowing it was inevitable, didn't hesitate and went straight up to Mr Dunbar's office. This was the first time she'd entered it since the day she had come looking for a job. Now things were very different and she felt she was about to be sacked. The very inevitability of this gave her courage.

'What is it?' Mr Dunbar looked over his spectacles at her as if she was an insect.

'Please, Sir, Mrs McCrudden sent me because I asked if I could return home as I feel poorly.'

Could she have heard right? Did she hear Mr Dunbar say, 'Well go home then, girl, if you must and mind you come early tomorrow' – or was she dreaming? No, they were his very words.

'Thank you, Sir,' she stammered, bobbed a curtsy, and went straight down to the cloakroom, fetched her outdoor things and left, leaving everyone – Mrs McCrudden included – to think that no doubt about it she had been sacked.

Why she had escaped the fate of all other workers who had dared to speak up for themselves at the laundry, Annie was never to discover. But she felt sure she had gained some sort of moral victory over Mrs McCrudden, however small, and had at least proved that she could survive the bullying she had received at her hands. Nonetheless, she didn't want to push things too far so she made it her business to report early the following morning, although she didn't feel at all well.

Annie wasn't to know that Mr Dunbar had received a threatening letter from the authorities hinting that he was contravening the sixty hours' work rule and he didn't wish to attract further unfavourable attention by dismissing another worker on the very day he had received the letter. Nor was Mrs McCrudden to know this, and she didn't make things easier for Annie the following day.

But the women were all obviously heartened to see that Annie had survived, and they crowded around her in the break, full of admiration for how she had handled the situation. They couldn't believe Mr Dunbar had let her go home without question.

Even Alice admitted that Annie had behaved courageously. 'We thought you would be dismissed,' she told Annie, looking at her with a new respect.

'I thought it myself,' admitted Annie. 'And thanks, Alice, thank you for trying to defend me from Mrs Mac.'

Somehow the incident raised the women's morale and again they discussed how they would go about joining a trade union. Even Alice seemed to favour the idea and at least didn't try and prevent them from talking about it.

'I know someone in the Knights of Labor who knows all about these things,' said Annie. 'I could get him to advise us how to go about it without getting us into trouble.'

Everyone thought this a good idea and Annie determined to waste no further time thinking about it but to approach Mike about it as soon as she could. But fate intervened only a couple of hours later, when something occurred at the laundry that was to settle everything for once and for all.

Shortly before four o'clock everyone in the basement became aware of a loud rumbling noise coming from the old coal boiler which was housed right next to the ironing hall. The janitor, a man who looked as old as the massive boiler, went to investigate; most of the women didn't even look up from their work to watch him do so.

The next thing they knew there was a massive explosion. The door of the boiler house flew open to reveal flames leaping everywhere and red-hot coals tumbling all over the floor. The janitor lay on the floor inside the door senseless, knocked down by the force of the explosion. No sooner had they glimpsed him than he was engulfed by flames and before they knew it smoke gushed towards the women as if in greedy pursuit of them.

Someone screamed, 'Run, run for God's sake'!

Pandemonium broke out instantly as everyone moved to react at the same time. As the smoke thickened the air and the lights were extinguished, people groped frantically to get to the stairs – the only exit from the basement. Suddenly everyone was coughing as the smoke reached their lungs. The confusion increased as women from the wash room, only now realising what had happened, began to converge on the ironing hall.

Annie felt she was suffocating. She couldn't understand what had happened. She panicked as she realised that in the dark she had lost her sense of direction and couldn't see where the stairs was. She couldn't breathe. Dear God, she couldn't give up, she must get out. A couple of women had fallen to the floor, overcome by the smoke. If only she could find the newel post at the bottom of the stairs, then she could feel her way upwards guided by the bannister rail. Women were groaning and calling for help, their voices breaking as the smoke invaded their throats. Trying to keep calm and pulling her overall over her face, Annie groped with her free hand and at last made contact with the staircase. Thank God. But ascending it was another matter. It was jammed with women, staggering from the effects of smoke inhalation and fumes. She pushed and pushed, dragging someone with her by the arm; she couldn't even see who it was. Why wasn't the door open? Was it locked? Panic overcame her again as she felt herself weakening and the woman she was pulling slipped from her grasp. All she was aware of was an overwhelming feeling of tightness in her chest before she lost consciousness.

Her mother's face swam in front of her, and she was overcome by a rush of sound like a wave crashing against the shore before receding. When Annie finally came to and opened her eyes she found herself in a white world – white ceiling, white walls, white door, white counterpane.

'Where am I?' She struggled to sit up but couldn't. Her mother gently pushed Annie back against the pillows, her familiar hand smoothing her forehead and hair.

'Shush darlin', it's all right. You're safe now. You're in the hospital.'

Suddenly it all came back, the smoke, the dark, the confusion, the heat and the awful panic as she felt herself losing consciousness.

'Where's Alice, where's Sophia?' She had forgotten that Sophia no longer worked at the laundry.

'Don't worry, Annie. It's all over now, do ye hear. It's all over. You're safe.'

Her mother's repeated words of comfort eventually worked their magic and when she awoke again it was to a clearer state of mind. She realised that she was in a hospital ward. Her bed, placed in the corner beside the window, was only one of many and all the beds were occupied. This time it was her father who sat guard beside her, and he started up anxiously to reassure her when he saw she was awake. She sat up suddenly with a fit of coughing, and he jumped forward with a glass of water.

Sipping it helped calm her and brought the realisation that her throat was acutely sore. But the relief of being able to breathe freely eased the pain.

'Father! What happened? How long am I here?'

'There's been a bad accident Annie, lass, but the doctors say you're fine, thank God.'

Then he pulled up his chair and gave his daughter an account of what had happened. She had no difficulty remembering the explosion but anything that happened after that was just a blank in her memory. It was just as well, her father reflected, looking at his daughter's smut-marked face and reddened eyes. How precious she was, he thought, thanking God again that she had been rescued. They could so easily have lost her.

Ten of the women had lost their lives, it came out, as well as the unfortunate janitor who had discovered the fire. Although the door at the top of the staircase had not been locked, it had a heavy iron latch that was difficult to lift at the best of times. Normally left ajar, the door was closed that afternoon as it was snowing heavily outside, and slush spilling in from the street tended to make the staircase dangerously slippy.

Overcome with smoke and rising panic, the women who had reached the top first took some time to lift the latch and open the door inwards against the press of women coming behind them. Most of those on the staircase then managed to escape or at least were rescued, but it was those left in the basement – many of them coming from the wash room and trying to get through the wall of flame that was steadily and mercilessly taking over from the smoke – who perished in the fire that then engulfed the laundry.

Most of the rescued women had been taken to the hospital next door, but some of the more critical cases were rushed by ambulance to the larger hospitals. The hook-and-ladder companies were quick to respond to the crisis, and the streets approaching the laundry were soon resounding with their warning bells as the firemen ran alongside the horses, shouting at other drivers to clear the way to the site of the accident.

Annie, who had been one of the lucky ones just suffering from severe smoke inhalation, was brought to St Mary's Hospital beside the laundry. The smoke had worsened her bronchitis, and she spent three days in hospital before being released. She discovered that Alice Rodgers and a number of the women in the ironing hall had also been treated there but many were released within hours. Alice, who had been kept overnight, had come to see her before she left. On seeing her, Annie burst into tears that were long overdue. Alice's arm was swathed in bandages and she looked pale and drawn, quite different from the strong, capable girl she had seemed at work.

'I'm fine, Annie, really. Don't fret so. You were very brave. Do you know you pulled Kitty Mulhall up the stairs with you to safety. If it wasn't for you she might not have made it.'

Annie learned that Mrs McCrudden had shown uncharacteristic kindness and nobility of spirit in the crisis and had stayed at the bottom of the stairs, trying to see that everyone got out. But sadly, she had been one of the ten women to perish in the fire and for all that she had suffered at her hands, this made Annie weep harder than ever.

'It's been written about in all the newspapers,' Alice

told her. 'Mr Dunbar is in real trouble. The laundry is finished now, and they say it will be closed down for good.'

Mixed with Annie's grief over those who had lost their lives was an overwhelming sense of relief that whatever else happened she would never have to work in the laundry again. She didn't know what she would do but nothing, she felt, could possibly be as bad as what she had experienced there.

Her spirits rose when she returned home to Monroe Street and the family cosseted her, the boys treating her like royalty. Tom came to visit and brought Mike, who presented her with a bunch of early daffodils.

'Why, I hear you saved Kitty Mulhall's life,' Mike said. 'Sure you're a pure heroine.'

'Don't believe it, Mike,' laughed Annie, knowing he was teasing. 'I don't remember anything about it and wasn't I lucky to be saved myself.'

'You had a narrow escape and no mistake about it,' replied Mike more seriously.

Her father shook his head sombrely. 'That Dunbar ought to be locked up,' he said.

'He won't escape scot-free anyway, that's certain,' said Mike. 'They were getting wise to him. He'll have to face the courts over this.'

When news got out that one of the Moores had been involved in the horrific fire at the Phoenix Laundry, the true spirit of the Lower East Side manifested itself among their neighbours, who showered them with kindness and support. Poor they may have been but never too poor to give help to one of their own.

Their Polish neighbour Mrs Walenski was guilt-stricken when she discovered that Annie was in hospital, as it was she who had suggested that she take the job in the first place. She had been a great support to Mother when the news came that Annie had been rushed into hospital. She took the boys and fed and looked after them, allowing Mother to fetch Father from the factory and get to the hospital without delay. The Petrowskis brought food to them when they returned from the hospital, and Mrs Rostov brought Annie a basket full of her delicious little poppy-seed cakes when she heard what had happened.

Sophia, of course, had been one of the first to know of the fire, as she had been working in the Bellevue Accident and Emergency section when some of the worst victims had come in. She had been frantic with worry about Annie until she had found out where she was and had got permission to go and visit her in St Mary's.

Molly had heard about it also. Reading the report in the newspaper it was her father who said, 'Isn't that where your young friend Annie works?'

She got such a fright that she called to the Excelsior Hotel that very day to ask Tom about it. Tom was able to reassure her that Annie was recovering but offered to bring her to see for herself at the earliest opportunity. Even Mr Abraham, the butcher Mother went to in the Hester Street market, sent round a grand cut of mutton with his compliments.

Annie made a full recovery and within a few days was even well enough to attend the funeral service for two of the women tragically killed in the fire. She returned home with a heavy heart, thinking of the needless loss of life caused by the unjust practices of one man.

She regretted that she had not been able to be more active in helping set up a trade union a little earlier but doubted if even that would have prevented the catastrophe from taking place. A strong sense of justice was awakened in Annie at this time, which was to last throughout her life.

13

RETURN TO ELLIS ISLAND

No longer having to work in the laundry gave Annie a freedom she had not had since coming to live in America. Of course she had to pay her way but luckily for her, Mike, who had been giving Mother some piecework from his company, turning collars and making buttonholes on gentlemen's jackets, was able to give Annie some work also just to bridge the gap until she found a good job in domestic service. She worked at home with Mother and did all the fetching and delivering from Mike's workplace. Annie liked this as it gave her a chance to get out and about and she saw much more of Mike than she would otherwise have done. The more she saw of him, the more she admired him and came to realise that he was an unusual and talented young man. Fund-raising for the Russian famine victims was the latest project that he had roped Annie and Tom into.

'You know, we Irish, of all people, ought to understand what it's like. My grandparents had terrible tales to tell about the Great Hunger in Ireland and how it all but ruined the country. The same thing is happening here. The

Russian refugees arriving here now are no different to our grandparents' generation – those of them who survived, that is. 'Twas so important to them to escape from Ireland in the late Forties that they gave their last penny just to get on one of those ships, not knowing rightly even what they were coming to. And as we know well, many of them perished on the way. There was no such thing then as the great steamships we came over on.'

Mike was speaking to a crowd of young people one evening at Tammany Hall. This time the occasion was the launch of a fund-raising campaign to help the many Russian refugees, many of whom were suffering – and many of whom had died – from typhus since their arrival. In some quarters they were blamed for the epidemic which had raged earlier in the year. Indeed it was reported in the newspapers that it was the Russians who had brought the typhus from famine-ridden Russia on the ships.

A total of 73,000 Russian emigrants had landed in New York in the year 1891, Mike told them. It was lucky that Sophia's family had left Russia well before the famine had caused such hardship, Annie thought, as she settled into her seat to listen. Tom and Molly were there to hear him too, along with many of those who had helped out at the presidential election campaign the previous Autumn.

Annie, who because of the demands of her work and her own bad health during the winter months, had had no opportunity for a social life, was delighted to see Molly again. She had already noticed that Tom and her new friend had got to know one another better, and she suspected that her older brother was by now a little in love with the lively, pretty trainee teacher from Brooklyn. He had already got to know her brothers through his activities at Tammany Hall, and Annie was sure it was no coincidence that he sought their company more these days in the knowledge that it would enable him to see more of Molly. She couldn't judge if her friend was equally taken with Tom but she hoped so. Molly was fun and friendly and forthcoming with most people she met, one of the reasons Annie enjoyed her company. But she knew Molly mixed with a lot of educated people who were a lot better off than they were and if it were not for their mutual interest in politics, her path and Tom's would probably never have crossed.

'The first event in the campaign will be a concert,' Mike was saying.

Annie's mind wandered again. She had noticed that her parents were a lot happier in recent times and put it down to the fact that Mother was feeling very well – the baby was expected in September – and that they were not quite as poor as they had been. She quite believed Father when he said that they might yet move west and buy a small plot to farm. She worried a little about them taking such an adventurous step with only Anthony and Philip to support them, but she wasn't ready to leave New York. The city, which only a year-and-a-half before had overwhelmed and frightened her, was now the most exciting place in the world to her.

She looked up at the podium where Mike was still speaking and sighed. She wished she were a few years older and maybe he would fall in love with her like Tom had with Molly. Maybe when she had found a new position he would no longer see her as his friend's young sister, or the helpless little emigrant girl he had helped on the voyage. He certainly seemed to have no other serious girlfriend, she reflected with relief.

Yes, they were still struggling to make a decent living and God knows it had been hard work. It had taken her parents four years to reach any kind of standard of living and Annie herself had swiftly come to know the meaning of hard work.

Annie knew that, like Tom, she would be expected to make her own way in the world and that the only way forward for her was to find a good position with a family. She was glad of the work from Mike, but she knew there were no prospects for her in that direction. She needed work that would give her enough to live on while she figured out what she might do with her life now that she was committed to staying in America.

'Annie, I've been to see Sister Bonaventure and . . . ' Mother was breathless, having climbed the stairs to their apartment at full speed and she already heavy with child. 'Oh, Lord, Annie, I haven't a breath left in me,' she gasped.

It was June already and the sun was beating down on the Lower East Side. Annie worked at the fully open window, the blinds drawn against the heat. She put down her work and brought Mother a drink of cold water from the faucet right away. 'What is it, Mother? What were you saying?'

'It's Sister Bonaventure, Annie. I believe she might have a position for you at last.' Mother paused, gulped the water gratefully. 'She was telling me about the Van der

Leuten family. They live near Central Park. They've a townhouse there. It's seems they're looking for staff. They rang the convent looking for respectable Irish girls and you're to go and see her. She might be able to recommend you. Wouldn't that be grand?'

Annie was very excited at this news. At last something was going to happen. She was sure of it. 'When should I go to see her?' she asked.

'The sooner, the better,' said Mother.

As soon as Annie had finished her work and tidied herself up, she set off for the convent. Sister Bonaventure was helpful and full of advice. It would be best if Annie applied for the parlourmaid vacancy. She was very inexperienced, after all, and it wouldn't do to appear too ambitious. She would learn more if she began, not at the bottom of the ladder which would be scullery or kitchen maid but in a position where she could learn the ropes from senior staff. Annie agreed. She had given very little thought to the nature of the work she would be required to do, but she was sure she could cope. Nothing after all, could be as bad as working in the laundry.

The only disadvantage was that if successful she could not take up the position until September. The Van der Leutens, it appeared, were about to leave New York for Newport, Rhode Island, not far from Boston, where they owned a summer residence. They would not return until the end of August.

'But I would be very happy, Annie, to recommend you for the position. I think you will be a credit to your family,' Sister Bonaventure said, smiling. Annie danced home, delighted with herself. Wait until she told Mother.

But when she got home she could see that Mother, while pleased at her news, was preoccupied with something else. She looked quite excited herself.

'Annie, I've got some news too. Very good news. You're going to be very surprised.' In her hand Mother held a letter. Annie held her breath.

'I didn't tell you anything because until now I wasn't sure and Father said not to upset you unnecessarily, but... well, see for yourself.' Mother handed Annie the letter.

Dear Mary and Matt

I am happy to tell you that we've been able to book a passage on the S.S Arizona, leaving Queenstown on the 15 July, and hope to arrive in New York on the 25th. I can't tell you how much we're looking forward to seeing you all and to a great new life in America.

Annie read no more of Auntie Norah's letter but let out a great whoop of delight, throwing her arms around her mother and dancing her around the kitchen. 'When did you hear... do the boys know... where will they live?' A thousand questions sprang to her lips but of one thing she was sure. She couldn't have had any better news than this. How marvellous it would be altogether to have dear Uncle Charlie and Auntie Norah with them in America. No wonder her parents had seemed happier lately.

'Stop, Annie, stop,' cried Mother, laughing as she was whirled around the room.

'But you're planning to go farming in the west. What

about . . .?' she began, but Mother was smiling and suddenly she realised that there had been a lot of planning going on that she knew nothing about.

When the boys returned from school that afternoon they had to be told and they greeted the news with equal joy. That evening the family sat down together and made plans. They would have to find somewhere for Charlie and Norah to live. It would be some time yet before they could move out of New York with Matt, Mary and the boys. They would have to find work and save hard for at least a year first. But that would suit, Mother said, as she and Father would not be in a position to take such a step until the new baby was at least a year old.

'Will Uncle Charlie be able to take me bowling again?' asked Philip, his eyes wide.

'No, but you can take him to a baseball match,' replied Father laughing.

On the morning of 25 July, the Moore family set off early for Ellis Island, retracing the steps they had taken on New Year's Day 1892. The SS *Arizona* was due to dock at about one o'clock and they wanted to be in good time to welcome their beloved aunt and uncle. Annie remembered well how she had felt on arrival, how overcome she had been when she got her first glimpse of New York and saw the Statue of Liberty as they sailed into the new Ellis Island terminal. She now knew what a big step it was for people to come out to America from Ireland and what great differences there were between the two countries. She had hoped and believed that it would turn out right and it had. No, the streets weren't paved with gold and you sure had to work very hard, but it was worth it all.

'Give me your tired, your poor, your huddled masses yearning to breathe free,' she recalled Emma Lazarus's lines. Yes, that was it – 'yearning to breathe free'. Now she understood at last.